DESIDERIUM

An Anthology

COMING FEBRUARY 2022:

DEAD OF WINTER: An Anthology

Presented by Dublin Creative Writers Cooperative

*Be the first to hear about our next anthology, DEAD OF WINTER,
and receive monthly writing and publishing tips in your inbox!*

HTTPS://WWW.DUBLINCREATIVEWRITERS.COM/BLOG

DESIDERIUM

An Anthology

Presented by
The Dublin Creative Writers Cooperative
Dublin, Ohio

SPARK
STREET
MEDIA

Published by
SPARKSTREET MEDIA LLC
HTTP://WWW.SPARKSTREETMEDIA.COM/

PO Box 3155
Dublin, Ohio 43016

DESIDERIUM: An Anthology

Presented by The Dublin Creative Writers Cooperative
Dublin, Ohio

Cover Design & Illustration
Copyright © 2021 Olga Begak

Curated by J. Powell Ogden

Edited by
Marília Bonelli
Gabrielle Gold

Copyedited by
Maddie Ogden

Interior Design and Formatting by We Got You Covered Book Design
WWW.WEGOTYOUCOVEREDBOOKDESIGN.COM

Paperback ISBN: 978-0-9989551-9-3
Ebook ISBN: 978-1-7376609-0-3

Grateful acknowledgement is made for permission to include both print and digital copies of the following stories in this anthology. All authors listed below retain full rights to their work, including the right to publish and reproduce them in print, digital or in any other form.

TABLE OF CONTENTS

"There is the heat of Love, the pulsing rush of Longing, the lover's whisper, irresistible—magic to make the sanest man go mad."

Homer, The Iliad

PRESENTS

The Dublin Creative Writers Cooperative (DCWC) is back with its second collection. *Desiderium: An Anthology* features a wide variety of poems and short stories, from flash fiction to a novelette, written by members of the group. Some works were crafted from the start with this anthology in mind, others originated as entries in our monthly writing contests, and a select few are hidden gems dusted off, polished, and brought to life anew.

As a group, the DCWC emphasizes the inclusion of both emerging and established writers. Whether authors' stories or poems were their first, second, or twentieth published piece, our goal was the same: a final product that would both entertain our readers and hone our skills. To that end, many hours of brainstorming, writing, editing, and much wrangling of ever-expanding spreadsheets (a hearty thank you to the project managers within our ranks!) went into crafting this anthology, and we are excited to share the results of our efforts with you.

Desiderium—an ardent longing, as for something lost—took us places we did not expect. Perhaps we should not have been surprised at the breadth of ideas and themes explored. After all, to yearn for something lost or missing is such a raw and fundamental human emotion; it encompasses everything from anger and fear to envy and deep, abiding grief. Members were given only "desiderium" as their theme to faithfully apply or warp as they saw fit. In this anthology, you will find fantasy, horror, Greek and Norse mythology, alternate history, and dystopian and heartfelt fiction. Poignant and harrowing themes included the pandemic, futuristic hacking, new relationships and dying lovers, joyful and bitter reunions, apocalyptic calamities and farewells. Hope, humor and tears.

We hope this anthology provides you with an escape from the everyday, in whatever flavor you prefer and, as always, thank you for supporting our authors and our work.

GABRIELLE GOLD
J. POWELL OGDEN
Editorial Board Members
July 2021

THE SUPER MASSIVE AWESOME PLAN FOR WORLD DESTRUCTION

By Marília Bonelli

THE END OF THE world lived in a recycled jam jar atop a bookshelf, stashed between a blue dragon made of tin and a cat that was really a pen. Or maybe it was a pen that was really a cat.

There could be no more innocuous hiding place for it to bide its time, multiply and grow until it was ready to do what it had dreamed of doing since the first sentient cell had come to life on a forgotten clump of decaffeinated coffee. Well, what *they* had dreamed of doing. They were a community, of course—a colony, one might say.

Years went by like that, except for a brief interlude when their jar went from shelf to box, rattling in a car as trees and blue skies went past—oh, how they wished they could contaminate it all—until they were made to sit still on a dresser, staring at an ugly brown couch. Then back to the car and back to their original shelf they went.

3

Finally, the day came when they were ready. The black sheen covered with the fuzzy white overlay was just the right color, like a sprinkling of snow on asphalt shining beautifully in a ray of sunlight, the perfect combination of color and texture to entice the unsuspecting mind. But unsuspecting persons rarely came.

They would invariably get their hopes up when visitors wandered their way while looking at the mismatched array of orange blobs—totems to the gods of some Hallows' Eve—on the shelf below and pick up their jar. Often enough, an amused expression would appear on their huge, distorted faces as their hands rested on the lid. So close…

"What the hell?" they would say. "Why do you have a jar of mold?"

"Beautiful, isn't it?" was the usual response.

Alas, beauty truly was a curse.

Sometimes, the visitor's touch would linger longer than usual on their prison, their hand grasping the lid a little tighter, and the colony's anticipation could almost make them—literally— burst. But then, food would distract their tentative liberators. It was always food.

The only one who kept the community company was the one who had locked them in the jar in the first place. Oh, she would admire them from time to time, but, as if she knew their plans, she never touched the lid. The one they'd once viewed as their unwitting accomplice had become their warden.

After all, if the lid didn't open, how were they to go out and destroy the world?

And why would fungi want to destroy the world, you may ask?

Well, why does a hurricane wish to flatten anything in its path? Why do wildfires desire to turn everything to ash?

Destroying the world—could there be any nobler purpose for a deadly black fungus? It was no more, nor less than their calling.

This calling had been discovered, of course, by their leader. The oldest of the fungus and thus technically their great-great-great-great-great-great-great-great-great-great-grandparent. Perhaps because it had been sitting on top of scribbled biology notes for longer than the others had been alive, it knew a few things.

This bout of learning came during the enlightened times of their existence, also known as the Paperweight Phase, which came after the primordial dark ages known as the Forsaken at the Back of the Cupboard Phase.

And so, after their enlightenment, they lived in misery for a while, always hopeful their fate would be fulfilled.

Then, one day—one beautiful, perfectly cloudy day—their would-be savior came!

Dressed in a wonderful beige color, with large wandering eyes and a disregard for all things breakable, the fungi knew it was only a matter of time before she released them.

They watched in helpless anticipation as she dusted the cabinet on the other side of the room, and then with fascination as she knocked a little glass sculpture in the shape of a flower onto the floor. Burning with jealousy, they were mesmerized by the sight of the shattered glass as it was unceremoniously swept away and thrown into the garbage.

They would have sighed wistfully—if sigh they could. Why couldn't that be their destiny, too?

When at last it was time for their own shelf, they focused all their attention on the elusive cloth-wielding hand. It came so close at one point that the more attentive fungi on the far side of the jar could actually see the specks of dust on the cloth.

Sadly, as quickly as it came, it was gone. A faint brush of outermost layer of cloth against the side of the glass, not even long enough for all the wistful little fungi to catch, and it was over. The hand withdrew.

"No, no! Come back, there's still more dust on the other side of the jar!" they shouted to no avail.

Once again, they had given up hope. It seemed today was not fated to be the day of their long-awaited liberation either.

And then, unexpectedly, their would-be savior dashed past them, the broom handle in her hands doing a magnificent 180-degree maneuver. Their savior disappeared out the door, rushing toward the food burning in the kitchen, but she had fulfilled her role!

Knocked over onto its side, off the jar went, rolling slowly along the shelf toward the edge. Eagerness and euphoria combined to slow their roll to an excruciating eternity. In that eternity, they dreamed beautiful dreams of world destruction. Maybe they would kill all the animals and maybe even the trees. Maybe they would kill the entire world.

"Freedom!" they shouted as the jar rolled off the edge. Such a wonderful feeling of falling into nothingness, with all their dreams waiting on the other end.

What had been a colony of silence now broke out into various cheers and exciting plans.

"We'll travel the world!"

"We'll go to a warm place! No, warm will dry us out."

"A cold place… But then cold is also dry."

"Near the beach then!"

"Near the beach!" they all cried.

"Yes! Eighty percent humidity and temperate climate!"

"Wait! Isn't that where we already live?"

"Shut up and pay attention! Nobody who's not making plans for destroying the world gets to speak!"

The eldest fungus—Fungus Maximus—continued his verbose descriptions of the strategy for the impending doom of the world. Though the plan was basically to go out into the world and multiply, the others weren't paying attention. They were simply shouting '*Whee!!!*' at the top of their imaginary lungs as their glass prison continued its long fall.

The floor was fast approaching. No one would be able to stop them now.

Plop.

Plop?

What happened to crash? What happened to shards of glass splattering across the ceramic floor? What happened to freedom?

It took the confused fungi a while to understand what had happened, mainly because the bottom of the colony, which had been flipped upside down, was now staring upwards at their shelf and the top half of the colony, now looking downwards, could only make out something encompassing half the jar.

The intact glass jar sat perfectly nestled in a forgotten pile of clothes that was being sorted to go into the washer.

And that's how dirty laundry saved the world.

A WINTER TO REMEMBER
By A. Howitt

SOME THINK THE GODS' very lives are glory—blood marring the edges of gleaming weapons, heroes so mighty the skalds weep to tell their tales, all-powerful and wise deities who disseminate the worlds' secrets in terrifying voices—their wills done by lesser beings.

From my perch, things look very different.

If ever there was a time that I pitied my one-eyed master, it was as I watched his vacant expression and the trail of crusted saliva tracking from the corner of his mouth. The sight might have affirmed to any of the other Aesir that the old man's time was up.

My brother Hugin was gone—vanished in the wee hours of the morning thirteen days earlier. The Allfather hadn't moved since. Reduced to a doddering fool, he was unable to even wipe away the dust collecting on the wide brim of his hat.

A blizzard raged outside Valaskjalf, our grand hall thatched in silver. From its tower, upon the great throne Hlidskjalf, Odin kept watch over the nine realms.

He watched no longer. As snow blanketed Asgard, the deranged Allfather stared at bird droppings on the arm of his throne, apparently captivated by the contrast of dark to light.

Hugin's absence left him as empty as a war drum. Without my brother to feed new thoughts into his head, the old man had been lost in a dream-state of his past. Beyond anyone's reach. Competent as I am, I cannot function as Odin's memory *and* thought.

For seemingly the hundredth time that morning the embalmed head on our breakfast table spoke an ominous warning. "Someone approaches. A pretty visitor."

"Shut up, Mimir," I said. "I can't think with your constant interruptions. If you keep bothering me, I'll throw you from the window."

"You can't lift me, puny bird," the massive head said.

"I'll start with your eye. Revenge for the one the Allfather paid for a look in your well. I'll pluck it and throw it in the snow. You can even have it back if you can find it."

"Munin," a woman scolded as she entered the Allfather's chamber. "Behave yourself."

Her swaying hips had a ruinous effect on males of every kind. Jotnar, dwarves, elves…even a god or two or a dozen succumbed to her charms. Weak, distractable fools.

"Freyja," I said, in what I meant as an unfriendly tone. Human voices are hard to mimic, their nuances many. Odin might have gifted us with speech, but he never took our anatomical limitations into consideration. Evidence of his selfish reason for bestowing the gift in the first place.

"I've looked in on our friends in the other realms," she said to the Allfather. "A month of hunting and feasting, drinking and boasting." Without Odin to interrupt, Freyja babbled on about the unpleasant business she faced being pretty and popular. It gave me time to come up with a few astute insults. Hers was an arrogant sort of beauty—factitious and self-serving. The vanity that went with it needed constant tempering. She stopped speaking and waved her hand in front of his pallid face. "What is this?"

"He always looks this way when he's cleaning his teeth."

Her head tilted, and I realized she missed my sarcasm.

"What do you think it could be?" I asked, cursing my lack of lips and the sneer that might have accentuated my words.

She shrugged, her falcon-feather mantle sliding off of one shoulder. "Is he ill?"

"It's a shame the Vanir didn't place a higher value on wisdom."

"Between you and that lewd lump on the table, it smells like this room is brimming with wisdom. You may want to open the shutters."

She knelt at Odin's side and took his hand. "What's happened to you, Wanderer? What keeps you in this place?"

I was taken aback by her authentic concern. "My brother. He hasn't returned for almost a fortnight."

"He's stuck like this until Hugin returns?"

"He's not defenseless if that's what you're asking," I said, ruffling my feathers. Her kind fell hard after the war, speaking of peace but secretly mourning their passing into the shadows of

Odin's stone throne. The Vanir, while not as strong as the Aesir, were still dangerous. They had a way of getting what they desired.

"I came to help, Munin," she said, removing the brooches clasping her magical mantle to her dress. "He asked for my cloak. I'm not here to push his limp form off that slab and spit on his corpse."

"I see you've given the Allfather's death some thought."

She scowled and set the feathered garment on the step. Odin made no sign of noticing. "I didn't delay my return to Folkvangr and the company of my fine warriors to be insulted by a plague bird. Perhaps I'll ask the dwarves to craft a tiny muzzle."

Sure, half the battle-slain lived on for eternity in Freyja's peaceful meadow—one of her favorite things to mention—but I liked to think they envied the other half who came to live in Odin's mead hall, Valhalla. Too bad I didn't think to mention it before she patted the old man's arm and called over her shoulder as she left, "Watch him, Munin. If word gets out, he'll have more to worry about than wine stains on his tunic."

I flapped up to my master's shoulder as she departed, taking my usual perch, so my words might reach the Allfather's mind, wherever it was. "Hugin will return." I'm not sure I believed it myself. Whatever was keeping my brother, it was killing the Allfather. "Imagine the wealth of knowledge he'll have for you."

The garrulous head snickered on the table.

"Your timing and humor are infantile, Mimir."

He snorted and guffawed, casting me a baleful glare. While the grotesque severed head gave Odin wise counsel, the slain jotun only sought to torment me.

I don't know if birds, even magical ones, possess anything similar to the quality humans call patience. I can be quiet. I can wait, watch, listen. But when there is a need, some drive within me, no amount of effort can subdue it. I needed the Allfather back. I needed Hugin.

Before I could even hurl an insult to quiet Mimir's laughter, the tower door opened again, and in marched a pair of brothers who only ever complicated matters.

The hulking brute with the hammer stomped in first, his wild red mane and beard making the furious gleam in his eyes more frightening. The other, lean and fair, followed. His braids swayed from side to side as he kept pace.

"Injustice," the Thunderer roared, his booted feet leaving noticeable imprints on the stone floor. "He's gone too far this time!"

"Who has?" I asked.

Thor rested his hammer on his shoulder and set his jaw, leaving Tyr to explain. "Thor is upset with Loki."

"Who isn't? The wolf father's jests are annoying, and he's out for revenge after the trick played on his son." My gaze settled upon the stump of Tyr's missing hand. "You well know the price of keeping Fenrir locked away."

"He appeared to Sif when she was bathing!" Thor shouted, a storm in his eyes. "An insult I won't tolerate."

Tyr, wise and brave, said, "If you go after Loki alone, you'll give him the advantage. Would you chase a bear into its den?"

Thor turned on his brother. "You already wear the rack of the bested stag. I'll die before I allow Loki to fit horns on my head."

Ravens mate for life. Humans and gods pretend to. I have only my brother for companionship, but I understood. Odin once pined for Freyja, and at the same time, he loved his wife Frigg dearly. Thor's insult struck like a hammer blow to Tyr, whose wife, Loki insisted, had borne him a son, one of the wise god's brood. "Enough!" I cried, wondering how mediating their sibling squabble fell to me. "Your father is in no position to offer counsel!"

They went silent and seemed to notice for the first time that Odin's solitary eye hadn't blinked since they arrived.

"What's happened to him?" Tyr asked.

Needing a moment to decide how much truth to tell, I pretended to preen my black feathers. "He's indisposed."

"A fine time for a spirit journey," Thor said. "While he searches for answers to useless questions, the wolf father runs amok—with our wives!"

Tyr's face became a pained grimace, so for his benefit, I relayed the tale. "We visited Vafthrudnir, speaker of fate, and the next morning Hugin left. He hasn't returned. Thirteen days. An inauspicious number. I fear this day may be the Allfather's last."

"What did he ask of the wise jotun?"

"He wanted to know whether Fimbulwinter had started, the terrible winter that foreshadows the end."

"He thinks Ragnarok has begun?" Tyr shook snow from his blond mane and braids. His light eyes searched the stony, solemn face of his father as if Odin's vacant expression might reveal some insight. "What did Vafthrudnir say? Is it the end? Ragnarok?"

"I don't know."

Thor swung his hammer Mjolnir in a wide arc and turned on his heels. "End or not, if Father can do nothing to stop Loki's games, I will do it!"

I flew to the window, knocking open the shutter to watch him go. It wasn't difficult to imagine why the Allfather feared the worst. With Asgard barely visible through the snow, it certainly looked like the great winter might have begun—setting off a series of events that would lead to the gods' final battle.

"Could this be one of Loki's games?" Tyr asked.

"Surely, it could be a game—just another mean trick between old friends," I said, considering for the hundredth time the implications of my brother's absence. With Odin reduced to a rather hideous piece of furniture and Thor out for blood, our family was fracturing already. "But, if there should be a fight over Odin's throne, Asgard would put up little resistance to a jotnar invasion."

He scratched his shaved chin. "My brother is gone. What else was said when the Allfather met with Vafthrudnir? Did he say what would happen to us?"

The riddle weaver's words echoed in my mind, and I recounted them for the wisest among the Aesir. "Only two people will survive Ragnarok. Lif and Lifthrasir—life and love of life. They'll survive by hiding within Yggdrasil, drinking the morning dew for sustenance, and repopulate the world of men." It reminded me of the first time, the dawn of man when Odin created Ash and Elm, the first humans.

"You believe that means we'll all perish?"

I wasn't sure what the mysterious words meant in regard to the future of the gods, but it was clear mankind was on the losing end of the final battle. "I don't know."

Cursing my limitations, I yearned for my brother.

But I was alone. "You know I can't see the future."

The severed head smiled smugly under a heavy brow and bulbous nose. Waiting for any opportunity to prove how wise he was and what an idiot I was.

"Wait. I may not be able to speak of prophecy, but *he* can." I flew across the chamber, landing before the slain jotun.

"Well-keeper," Tyr said, "you have the sight."

Cheeky Mimir frowned. "Munin forbade me to speak."

"The God of Wisdom revokes the forbidding."

"Forever?" Mimir and I asked at the same time.

"Sure."

The head laughed in my face, an assault of embalmed breath. "Did you hear that, Munin?"

"No," I said.

"Please, Mimir," Tyr said. "Tell us, has the end begun?"

The slain jotun frowned thoughtfully. "If you wouldn't mind putting it in writing—"

I scrambled up the head, not minding where my claws landed, and peered directly into his huge left eye. "Answer, or I'll see for myself." I pressed my beak against the socket—just enough pressure to hurt. Even I wouldn't risk damaging such an eye without good reason.

"Fine!" Mimir shouted. Unable to defend himself, he blinked rapidly. "I'll tell you!" He attempted to shake me loose. "Get off of me!"

I hopped down to the table confident my point had been made.

He stuck his dark tongue out at me. "In the end of times, all Asgard will lay in ruin, burned by the fiery residents of Muspelheim. Valhalla will be destroyed, and the Aesir will fight a war to end all wars. Fenrir will break free and swallow Odin."

One of my eyes watched the wise god cradle his stump upon hearing of the wolf's freedom. The other noticed Mimir's troubled wrinkles.

"The Midgard Serpent will unfurl as the world floods. The ship *Naglfar* will transport legions of jotnar to confront the gods in the final battle."

He opened his eyes again. "Only a few will survive. I cannot see their faces."

"Has it begun?" I demanded.

His eyes rolled to the ceiling, and he tilted back. For a brief moment I got a frightening view up a giant nostril. "No."

"So, where is my brother?"

He scowled. His eyes crossed in order to see me clearly. "If I tell you, will you never again threaten to steal my eyes?"

"Fine."

"And laugh at my jokes?"

"What?"

"I can't leave this tower. We never have visitors." He pouted in a way that employed eyes, and lips, and chin. His whole face. "Geri and Freki growl at me."

"Fine, fine, I will laugh at your stupid jokes!"

"And not call them stupid," he added in a mumble.

I flapped my wings because I lacked a fist to punch him. "Yes! All of it!"

His face stopped begging, and his eyelids closed, twitching as he searched his undoubtedly complicated mind.

I grew impatient. Mimir finally opened his eyes again. "He's in Jotunheim, past the river Ifing, in the shadows of Utgard."

I recognized the name Utgard. Home of the great trickster Skrymir, who once cheated Thor out of winning a drinking contest by giving him a magical horn that filled from the ocean.

"You will find the raven in a golden cage beside a pond deep within a cave."

Mimir's solemn tone set my feathers bristling. Captured? My brother needed me. I hopped onto the back of a chair facing the open window.

Tyr spoke up. "Wait, Munin. I'm coming with you."

"The Allfather is dying. I'll be faster alone, without worrying about your bodily limitations." I cringed. "Not because of the hand thing." I hastened to the window. "You can't cross the river. Its roiling waters kill any that enter."

The storm raged outside, a mix of hail and howling, the worst of winter all at once.

"You'll need me, Munin."

Something in his tone convinced me he might be right. The

18

God of Wisdom was no fearmonger. One doesn't maintain a position at the Allfather's side and not learn a thing or two about the gods' uncanny ability to find and predict trouble. The realm of the jotnar was a perilous place, and I was only a collection of Odin's memories.

"I'll fly over the river with you." He lifted Freyja's magical falcon cloak, draping it over his shoulders.

Every moment my brother was gone was a moment longer our master had half his mind. It would be worse when I left. Only I could find poor Hugin, and without human conveniences like thumbs I was better off with the wise god at my side.

"Watch after him, Mimir," I said, putting as much gravity as I could muster into my tone. With Geri and Freki, Odin's two wolves, snoring on the floor, Tyr and I set out.

We soared over a hibernating Asgard to the realm of Jotunheim. Whiteness spread to the reaches of my sight. Endless sheets of sleet assaulted my head and wings. I beat harder, pulling strength from my core, where love for my master and brother warmed my very soul, driving me onwards. My brave companion followed without complaint, though I suspected his naked limbs fared worse than mine. I was built to weather winters, after all—just not ones so wholly dismal.

We passed over the river between worlds, where the water ran in a torrent so violent it never froze. Before us stretched a vast snowy wasteland where life fought to survive in the region's best conditions. In the distance loomed foggy mountains and the foreboding stronghold Utgard. Dark walls of stone thrust

19

upward from craggy hills.

With keen sight, I searched for a cave. Struggling with the fading sun's glare against the snow and wind, I cursed with every breath. With the wise god following, I searched up and down bleak crags until I spied it, a rocky outcropping split by a dark crevice.

We landed at the cave mouth and Tyr entered, sword in hand. I perched upon his shoulder, unable to fly in the confines of the narrow passage and ill-equipped for a trek on foot.

"Direct me, Munin," Tyr said. "I can't see five feet in this darkness."

It was a struggle for me too, but I didn't want to delay. I relayed what I could see, guiding Tyr through the passage. Dreary blackness gave way to dim light, emanating from stray crystal shards scattered throughout the cavern and an adjoining chamber—a rainbow shattered and strewn about the ugliest place I'd ever seen. And I've seen the underworld, where death is a kinder sight than Hel, Loki's somber daughter, herself.

A rumble in the murky darkness, and then another. Something moved in the depths of the foreboding cave. Something big.

"I hear something," I said.

"I hear it too! The wolf stole my hand, not my ear." Tyr's muscles bunched and flexed under my feet.

"What do you suspect it is?"

"A guardian." Tyr moved like a cat stalking prey.

"Interesting Mimir didn't mention it. I mean, he was quite specific about the golden cage and other details."

"Be quiet," Tyr hissed, drawing his sword.

The rumble grew closer, jarring rock and crystal shards from the walls and ceiling. I readied myself for flight. I'm smart, not brawny. My battle preparation consisted of remembering the way to the exit.

A great serpent's head darted from the depths. Tyr brought his weapon to bear. Green-gray scales glistened in the faint light.

Instincts honed, Tyr dodged a bite from the gaping maw filled with pointed teeth. He swung his sword overhead in a wide arc, striking the scales. A metallic ring shattered the stillness of the cavern, larger than our tower chamber and taller than two men.

With a frantic fluttering of wings, I spread distance between the serpent and myself, glad then to have as my companion the only god whose strength rivaled Thor's. While the Thunderer was acknowledged as the strongest among the Aesir, Tyr's bravery was unmatched.

The two exchanged blows, shaking the earth. Tyr struck, narrowly avoiding a fierce bite, and swung again, jarring scales free of the serpent's neck. Green blood oozed, filling the chamber with a sickly odor like wet mushrooms and soured wine.

A vicious hiss and the weakened creature lashed out again, coiling its tail to put weight behind a clumsy strike. The movement was slow, predictable. Tyr sidestepped and slapped the side of the serpent's head with the flat of his blade.

He could have slain the monster.

I alighted upon a nearby stalagmite and watched, curiosity being as much a part of my nature as the hoarding of secrets.

Using his stump to hold the scaled head against the ground,

Tyr pressed his sword point between the missing scales on the creature's neck. "Surrender or I'll slay you, servant of the trickster god. Are you willing to die for him?"

The serpent let loose a sibilant hiss, its gleaming eyes wide. "I yield."

Tyr stood, allowing the serpent to rise if only a few feet. It dragged its weight up into a docile coil and focused slit eyes on the one-handed god. "I s-s-serve no tricks-s-ster, glorious-s-s lord. What command have you for me?"

"A life for a life," Tyr said. "I'll spare your life, expecting it shall be given one day when asked for."

The serpent bowed, if that's even possible. It looked like a clumsy bow, anyway. Generous-s-s lord, my life is-s-s yours-s-s."

Tyr evidently accepted the serpent at its word, because he sheathed his sword. "If you do not work for Loki, what are you doing here?"

"I live here, collecting beautiful things-s-s in my cavern."

"We should move on," I said, returning to Tyr's shoulder.

"You have a bird in a gold cage," Tyr said.

An angry hiss escaped the serpent. "Yes-s-s. A cruel trick."

"What trick?"

The crescent eye narrowed a touch. "An old woman traded the s-s-singing bird for my ruby mirror. But it will not s-s-sing."

"It was stolen. I've come to claim it for its rightful owner."

"It chatters-s-s, vomiting ominous-s-s warnings-s-s with a malicious-s-s tongue."

My heart rejoiced. It could be none other than Hugin.

"It looks-s-s like that one," the serpent said, "but s-s-smells-s-s better."

I took to the wing and headed down the passage, searching for my brother. In the next chamber, crystals emanated soft light that reflected off a still pool surrounded by assorted objects. Some of the treasures were easy to appraise as junk—tools and utensils.

On the ground near the pool sat a golden cage, just as Mimir described. A familiar dark shape was within.

"Hugin!"

Six locks of iron stood between us.

"Munin?" His head popped up. "I'm stuck!"

Tyr knelt to examine the locks.

"Here is-s-s the bird that cannot s-s-sing," the serpent said, joining us.

"Munin, you must bring a message to the Allfather."

"We're here to rescue you," I said. "Bring him the message yourself."

"Loki caged me to disrupt the Allfather's hold on Asgard. He seeks to release Fenrir."

Tyr tensed beside me. "You gave your word," he said to the serpent.

"I s-s-spoke truth!" It recoiled defensively. "Take the bird. I am your s-s-servant."

"How does he plan to release the wolf?" Tyr asked Hugin.

I felt sad for him. A shame it would be if he sacrificed his hand for nothing.

"I don't know. I doubt he can," Hugin said, "but the locks

are magical, so here I'm stuck." His voice was as weak as his spirit. "They cannot be opened with keys, or picked, or broken. An old and enduring magic. Not even with Mjolnir could they be cracked."

"Tyr is the wisest of the gods," I said. "He'll find a way to free you."

"Maybe the cage itself can be broken," Tyr said.

"It's bound to the magic of the locks." My poor brother drooped on his perch.

"How can we free you then?" I asked.

Tyr turned one of the solid iron locks over in his hand. "Loki must have fastened them somehow. How did he do it?"

"In a hushed whisper!" Hugin ruffled up until he was twice his normal size. "The secret of the locks are the six elements that went into creating Gleipnir, the ribbon that binds the wolf."

"The dwarves crafted it from things that don't exist," Tyr said. "How can we collect them?"

"We don't need the items," Hugin said. "They don't exist for a reason."

Tyr released the lock. "So, we must speak their names to open the locks?"

"Precisely."

"Easy enough," I said. "Why haven't you freed yourself?"

Hugin eyed the serpent and shrunk back down to normal. "I can't remember them."

"I don't know," the serpent said. "The old woman s-s-said only s-s-singing bird for rubies-s-s. Nothing of locks-s-s."

My eye met the wise god's. He shrugged and said, "I put my hand into the wolf's mouth. I don't know how the dwarves made the ribbon. I doubt even Freyja knows, and she was the one who convinced them to craft it."

"The sound of a cat's footfalls," I said.

A scratching creak and one of the locks came open.

For once, seeing only the past with keen meticulousness came in handy.

"The beard of a woman." Another latch opened.

"The roots of a mountain and the sinews of a bear," I continued. "The breath of a fish, and the spittle of a bird."

Tyr opened the cage door. Hugin flew out, freed from his bondage.

The serpent ducked and coiled. "Generous-s-s lord, you have your bird. And my oath. Let me keep the golden cage."

Tyr left the cage on the ground. "Live in peace, friend. We'll make sure that the old woman who fooled you pays for his treachery."

"We must return to Asgard," I said, imagining Odin slowly crumbling to dust in our absence. I wasn't ready to reveal all my theories to Hugin—at least not until we had a chance to speak privately. While he could make sense of almost everything he viewed, I was a collector of history, weaker at theorizing than interpretation. If Loki was indeed trying to free his vicious son, perhaps the time of the gods' final reckoning was closer than we feared. Mimir's assurance that the end had not begun comforted me only slightly as we left the serpent's cavern and soared above Jotunheim.

In the frail light of winter, we passed over the river Ifing again. My eye caught sight of something colorful beside the raging water. I disregarded it at first. When I spotted a second burst of color, my heart pounded faster. A green shoot peeked through the snow, the faint purple of a budding flower visible—the iris, one of Loki's sacred plants. It seemed winter was coming to an end after all. I just hoped I didn't owe Mimir an apology on top of my gratitude. Having to laugh at his jokes until he forgot my promise would be humiliating enough.

When we arrived in Asgard, it was a homecoming I didn't expect. A crowd gathered around the silver door of Valaskjalf. Thor, hammer in hand, with Freyja and her brother Freyr at his sides—a blazing red king flanked by two fair, blonde warriors in battle raiment. Concern painted their faces—enough to bring the Thunderer out of his rage and remind him that his father was an old man.

Hugin and I sped to the throne in the tower, using our window rather than the door blocked by those who protected the entrance of Odin's silver hall.

As if not a damn thing was wrong in the world, Odin stood from his seat upon Hlidskjalf and held out his arms, so we could find our places, one at each ear—as it had always been.

The skalds will forever tell tales of Odin's glory. They'll praise his wisdom and valor until the end of time. His one-eyed face will be carved upon stone markers and talismans by men who make sacrifices to earn his favor. But none will ever speak of my journey. Over time, it will fade from the memories of Asgard's people, who would rather boast of their feats while spilling mead on the floor than acknowledge that one day the throne in the high tower of Valaskjalf will be empty.

One day the Midgard Serpent will unfurl, and the legions of jotnar will come, as Vafthrudnir portended. We will see who survives with Lif and Lifthrasir and who will rebuild Asgard when the Bifrost shatters.

I don't envy Mimir, who knows too much, or my brother, who constantly worries for the future. I am the keeper of secrets, collector of the past, and voice of the dead. The only one who knows how close Loki came to ending the Allfather, and me along with him. I'll always be what I've always been, until Odin's final breath. Except, now I must pretend to laugh when Mimir jests. Which isn't altogether difficult, I found out. He's an embalmed severed head. What isn't funny about that?

HOME FOR THE HOLIDAYS
By J. H. Schiller

THANKSGIVING

"THE END IS COMIN', friends." Reverend Sluss gripped the wooden pulpit and peered at the congregation over half-moon glasses. "We been seein' the signs, ain't we?"

Misty rolled her eyes. She'd only been to this church a handful of times, and on every occasion, she'd heard the same damn sermon. She'd hoped today would be different—maybe he'd get crazy and talk about gratitude or Pilgrims or, shit, flying saucers—but nope. More fire and brimstone. Misty had only a passing familiarity with the Bible, but she was starting to wonder if this joker read anything besides the end.

"We're in the last days, y'all. Can I hear Amen to that?"

A chorus of Amens and Hallelujahs drowned out her muttered response: "Bullshit."

Jack squeezed her hand and looked up at her from saucer-wide eyes.

Damn it. Through the smothering blanket of grief and the distracting buzz of anxiety, she hadn't even considered how this crap would sound to Jack. She should've known better than to bring him, but Mom and Dad had begged. They wanted to show off their only grandchild.

What had actually swayed her, truth be told, was the food. As evidenced by her contribution to the church's potluck Thanksgiving dinner (store-bought deviled eggs), Mom was no cook. The prospect of choking down dry turkey and instant mashed potatoes on their first Thanksgiving since...

Well, it wasn't all that appealing. On top of that, Mom and Dad were letting her and Jack stay with them rent-free until her new job in New York started at the beginning of April. A few months of sporadic church attendance had seemed a small price to pay.

"What does that mean, Mama?" Jack whispered. "What last days?"

"Don't worry, baby. It's not—"

"It's time for the feedin' of the lambs," Reverend Sluss said. "All you little 'uns, come on up here in front of the altar and take a seat. Miss Pat's got a sucker for you, but you can't open it 'til after I've shared the good Lord's word."

Jack released her hand and started to rise.

Oh, hell no.

Misty rested her hand on his shoulder and pressed him back down onto the cold wooden pew.

"But I want a lollipop, Mama." Jack craned his neck to watch the other kids settling in on the worn carpet.

"I'll get you something better."

"Go on up, Jackie," Dad said. He turned his knees to make room, and Jack popped up and snaked down the aisle before she could catch him.

"Damn it, Dad—"

"Mind your tongue, girl," he hissed. "This is God's house."

Misty only barely choked back an angry retort. When she was Jack's age, she'd spent her Thanksgiving alone in a forty-degree trailer eating SpaghettiOs out of the can while her parents drank their way through the coal camps. Of course, now that they'd seen the light and reformed their sinful ways, she was expected to pivot with them into full-blown evangelical insanity and forget everything that had gone before.

She would never forget.

Dad looked up at Jack, who was happily accepting a cherry blow pop from Miss Pat. "It ain't like he's off with strangers. You've known most o' these folks all your life." He pointed a leathery finger at the altar. "And he ain't but twenty feet away from you."

Misty shook her head but made no further protests. She was already spending her nights unpicking the knots of fear left in Jack's mind by witnessing his father's death. If these simple-minded fools threw the apocalypse into the mix, she'd unpick that too.

"Open up yer Bibles, kids."

Jack shifted uncomfortably and stared down at the floor.

"Where's yours at, son?"

Jack stared up at Reverend Sluss but didn't answer. His cheeks—even the tips of his ears—turned red under the scrutiny of the congregation. Misty started to stand up and go to him, but Dad grabbed her hand. *Please,* he mouthed. She knew what that *please* meant.

Please don't make a scene.

Please don't embarrass me.

Interesting. Where had all this concern for appearances been when he'd driven his pickup truck onto the football field during her high school graduation?

But she was staring down the barrel of four more months living with her parents. She decided to stay put. For now.

"You're Robbie Wright's grandson, ain't you?"

Jack clutched the blow pop and nodded.

Reverend Sluss propped his hands on his knees and leaned down closer to Jack. "Didja forget yer Bible at Papaw's house, son?"

Oh, here we go.

Jimmy, a lapsed Catholic, had sporadic conversations with Jack about God and the Bible and why they chose not to go to church. Misty had left him to it. She had nothing child-appropriate to say on the topic of organized religion. Now, she sat in the pew and held her breath, waiting to see how her son would respond.

"No, sir," Jack said. "I, um… I just don't have one."

Well, at least her son was a *polite* heathen.

Forty-odd heads swiveled to look at Misty. She kept her eyes trained on Jack, her expression carefully placid. She could feel her right cheek heating up under Mom's glare.

"That ain't hard to fix." Reverend Sluss straightened and caught the eye of Miss Pat, who was seated in the front row. She rose and scurried toward the back of the church. "And you know, young man, this ties right into today's scripture. Children, open your Bibles to the book of Ephesians, chapter six."

Miss Pat returned and handed Jack a black Bible. He stared blankly at the book, then up at Reverend Sluss.

"Braden, help him find the right page."

A boy with the reddest hair Misty had ever seen nodded and scooted closer to her son.

When the boys were ready, Reverend Sluss said, "Any of y'all like knights?"

Four of the five kids raised their hands. The outlier, a girl who couldn't have been more than three, stuck out her bottom lip and said, "I like princesses."

Reverend Sluss chuckled. "Well, we got princesses in the Bible too, darlin', but today, we're talkin' 'bout warriors." He opened his own Bible and glanced down at the page. "Read along with me, verse eleven. 'Put on the whole armor of God, that ye may be able to stand against the wiles of the devil.'"

Jack's eyebrows drew together in a confused frown.

The devil. Jimmy must not have covered that little theological gem. Perfect. Something else she'd be unpicking later tonight.

Reverend Sluss read the passage aloud to the children, describing the belt of truth, the breastplate of righteousness, the shield of faith, the helmet of salvation, and the sword of the Spirit. Then he closed his Bible and held it aloft. "This right here, now this is yer sword. The word of God. That's why—"

The floor lurched and started to shake, and the worn carpet rippled underfoot. Over a low, grating rumble punctuated with sharp cracks, Misty heard a handful of screams.

"Mama!"

At the sound of Jack's panicked voice, she staggered to her feet and stumbled into the aisle. Before she'd even taken a step toward the altar, the rumbling stopped, and the earth was still once more. Earthquakes weren't unheard of in eastern Kentucky, but Jack wouldn't know that. With this last days nonsense, he probably thought the world was ending.

She looked up, expecting to see the kids huddled together on the floor, crying in fear. Instead, they stood with their backs to the congregation. Their heads tipped slightly back as they gazed up at the wall behind the altar. Most country churches would have a simple wooden cross hanging there, but this one had a large banner that changed with the seasons, in front of which stood a freestanding cross on a pedestal. The banner had torn in two from top to bottom, revealing a starburst pattern of cracks that seemed—from her vantage point—to radiate out from the intersection point of the cross.

Reverend Sluss fell to his knees. "'And behold,'" he said, the harsh whisper of his voice breaking the shocked silence, "'the veil of the temple was torn in two from the top to the bottom, and the earth did quake.'"

Misty tried to go to Jack, to walk down the aisle to her son, but she couldn't move. Her body simply would not respond. The air felt thick and heavy, and the church was as silent as the grave. In the stillness, the children turned to face the pews.

"A pale horse…" The little girl's piping voice and mild lisp did nothing to detract from the eeriness of the moment. "A pale horse…"

"Rides from the east," said the redheaded boy.

"Sowing disease." That was *Jack*. She strained toward him but couldn't so much as twitch a finger. "Bringing pestilence."

The little girl said, "The pale horse…"

"Rides for the city." This girl was older, maybe eleven or twelve. "The city…"

"The sleepless city," said a boy who was clearly her brother.

The redhead whispered, "The city falls."

"The sleepless city…"

Jack said, "One thousand dead."

"Five thousand dead." The children spoke in unison now.

"Ten thousand dead."

"Fifteen…"

"Twenty…"

The earth shook again; then, as one, the children fell to the floor like marionettes whose strings had been cut.

"Jack!" Misty lunged forward, expecting to fight traitorous muscles, but her body responded almost eagerly, and she nearly fell. She regained her footing and rushed to the front of the church, where she knelt next to him. "Wake up, baby," she said. "Mama's here."

His eyelashes fluttered, and she patted his pale cheek. "Come on, Jackie." He didn't move.

Dad. She needed Dad.

He was a coal miner who had to stay current on his EMT training. He'd know what to do. She looked back, half expecting that he'd have followed her to make sure Jack was okay. But he hadn't. He was kneeling in front of his pew, his arms raised in what she had snarkily dubbed the Hallelujah Vee.

It wasn't just him.

Everyone, including Mom, was down on their knees with raised arms, rapturous faces fixed on the cross.

She looked helplessly down at the other kids. No parents were coming to check on them, to comfort them, to make sure they were all right.

"Brothers and sisters," Reverend Sluss boomed. Misty flinched at the sound of his voice. He struggled to his feet, keeping his arms held high, palms up. "We are witnessin' the fulfillment of His promise. The gospel tells us nation shall rise against nation, and there shall be famines, and pestilences, and earthquakes."

Misty tried her best to tune him out. She had to help Jack. She rested her hand on his chest. He was breathing fine, and his color was good. Why wouldn't he wake up?

"The Lord says our sons and daughters will speak prophecies at the end of days," the Reverend said. Misty felt the weight of his burning gaze as he looked down at the children. "My friends, it has begun."

To hell with this. Misty slid her arms under Jack's body and picked him up, then stood and hitched him higher, cradling him against her chest. He was so light… *too* light. He hadn't been eating well in the month since Jimmy died. She carried her son down the aisle toward the back of the church. Mom and Dad, totally caught up in Reverend Sluss's fervor, didn't even glance their way. She shouldered through the door at the back of the church and carried Jack into the fellowship hall, where the inviting smell of a home-cooked Thanksgiving dinner hung in the air.

"Mama?"

Relief coursed through her. "I've got you, baby." She carried him to one of the round tables and hooked the leg of a metal folding chair with her foot, dragging it out far enough that she could sit.

Jack squirmed free of her tight grip and sat up on her lap. He looked around the empty fellowship hall, then turned quizzical eyes up to her. "What happened? Why am I in here?" His eyes grew watery, and his voice quavered. "Where's my lollipop?"

"In your hand, silly," she said, blinking back tears of her own.

He looked down at his hand, frowning. When he saw the twisted top of the blow pop protruding from his fist, he broke into a sunny smile. "I *am* silly. Can I have it now?"

She smiled and nodded. It was a good thing he couldn't read minds. If he'd asked for a Mercedes and a Rolex, she'd have said yes. She'd already lost Jimmy. The thought of something happening to Jack was too much to bear. The needle of panic that had pierced her heart when he collapsed began to withdraw. But as it receded, questions popped up to fill the empty space— questions about what had just happened, what Jackie had said.

Pestilence? He'd never even heard the word, she was sure of it. What did it mean? Could it possibly be…

No.

Hell, no.

If there was a God, Misty wanted nothing to do with him. He'd taken Jimmy in a gruesome car accident that left their son soaked in his father's blood and so traumatized he hadn't spoken for a week. She'd just gotten Jack to the point where he could sleep through the night without screaming. The very last thing she needed right now was a fucking existential crisis.

Unfortunately, that didn't silence the voice whispering unanswerable questions in her head. What was it her therapist had said about dealing with a pattern of intrusive thoughts?

Don't give it any mental real estate.

Push it down. Push it away. Ignore it and focus on surviving until they could get the hell out of this godforsaken town.

The crunch of Jack chewing his lollipop derailed her train of thought.

"That's not good for your teeth, baby." Mom autopilot to the rescue.

He grinned up at her and chomped again. She returned the smile. God, she loved this kid.

God.

No.

"Did I fall asleep and miss the story?"

Her smile faded.

"The story about the knight?" He looked around. "And where's my Bible? The lady gave me one."

"I'm sure Papaw will bring it."

"He better hurry," Jack said. "The end is coming."

CHRISTMAS EVE

"Mama, there's no toilet paper!"

"Look under the—"

"I already did," Jack said. "There isn't any, and I really, really need some."

Yeah, Mom's cooking tended to have that effect.

Misty sighed and kicked the recliner's footrest back into the chair. She stood and looked down at her parents, who were snuggled on the couch under a crocheted afghan, watching *A Christmas Story* for the third consecutive time. "Where's the TP?"

"In the shed," Mom said, her eyes never shifting from the screen. "And grab that tin of butter cookies while you're out there."

"Will do." She stopped in the hall on her way out and knocked on the bathroom door. "Back in a sec, Jackie."

"It's okay," he said, "I brought a book."

Ah, he truly was his father's son.

Stupidly, the thought of Jimmy's marathon shits caused her eyes to fill with tears. Misty took a shuddering breath and wiped her eyes with the cuff of a truly heinous ugly Christmas sweater. She grabbed her dad's keys from a hook in the kitchen, then shrugged into her coat and jammed her feet into his snow boots.

It was Jack's first big snowstorm, and as much as she'd rather be anywhere but here, there was something uplifting about having a white Christmas. It felt personal, like it had showed up just for her and her son. Jack had been utterly delighted when the morning's flurries turned into knee-high drifts. He'd spent the afternoon in a hastily purchased Walmart snowsuit making a heart-shattering snow family.

Drooping evergreen branches on Jimmy's back had served as angel wings.

God, she missed him.

Misty closed the door behind her and looked up at fat, picture book snowflakes drifting lazily from the twilit sky. She tilted her head back and stuck out her tongue to catch one. Smiling, she slogged across the driveway's expanse of pristine snow to the shed she'd mentally christened the Crazy House. In the four weeks since Thanksgiving, Dad had converted his 10' by 16' garden shed into a doomsday prepper's wet dream. As she unlocked the door, her eyes landed on the sign her mother had hand-painted on the door.

It's TEOTWAWKI, and I feel FINE!

Yeah, well, the end of the world as Misty knew it had nothing to do with half-baked religious revelations and everything to do with a patch of black ice and a jackknifing flatbed semi.

She opened the door and flipped the light switch, above which her father's whimsical contribution was mounted—a glass-encased fire axe with a sign that said *Break in case of zombies.*

Har-de-fucking-har.

Though they made frequent end-of-the-world jokes, her parents took the Thanksgiving Revelation, as Reverend Sluss called it, very seriously. Mom had gone so far as to trot out *Everything happens for a reason*, insinuating that Jimmy's death was God's way of keeping her family from moving to New York in April. Misty had immediately started packing but, with no money, no car, and no place to go, their suitcases had never left the house. After a week of the silent treatment, Mom apologized. Misty pretended everything was fine, but the second Jimmy's insurance policy paid out, they were out of here.

When she and Jack arrived last month, the shed had been home to garden tools, a wheelbarrow, a lawnmower, and a couple of ancient bags of Quikrete. That was no longer the case. She scanned the floor-to-ceiling shelves. Row upon row of canned food. Tupperware containers full of seed packets. A fifty-pound bag of rice. Boxes of cereal and pasta. Jugs of water. Medical supplies, including prescription antibiotics and antivirals smuggled in from God knew where. A rack of guns and boxes of ammo. And, of course, the most critical item of all: hundreds of rolls of toilet paper. She grabbed four rolls and the requested blue tin of Royal Dansk Danish butter cookies.

Misty took a last look at the overflowing shelves. She fished her phone out of the back pocket of her jeans and snapped a picture, then attached it to a text.

Check this shit out, babe. Can't wait to GTF outta here!

Then she sent the message to Jimmy.

She still hadn't canceled his cell service, and she texted him every few days. She liked to imagine him grinning at his phone, then sending a string of spot-on emojis that would have her laughing her ass off. The whole thing was stupid, but it made him feel not quite so... so *gone*.

Her phone buzzed in her hand, and she yelped and dropped it.

Trembling from more than the cold, she stooped and picked it up. It couldn't be.

Could it?

If it was Jimmy, she'd tap dance to church every damn day playing "The Old Rugged Cross" on a fucking kazoo. She unlocked her phone and, with a shaking finger, tapped the unread text notification.

I don't know, Boots... I'm starting to think they're onto something.

Boots. Misty'd earned that nickname by streaking across the football field wearing only a pair of red cowboy boots after a boozy homecoming bonfire her senior year. (Apparently, the apple didn't fall far from the keg.) Only one person in her life called her that, and it wasn't Jimmy.

It was Jessie.

She must've texted Jessie by mistake.

Best friends since high school, they'd both dreamed of escaping Three Forks and moving away to the big city. Then Jessie's mom got colon cancer. While Misty left for the University of Kentucky on a full ride, Jessie worked at Hardee's and Magic Mart to keep a roof over her mom's head while she died a slow, painful death. By the time she was gone, it was too late to get out.

Jessie was twenty and pregnant. She'd stayed in their hometown, where she'd put herself through nursing school as she raised her daughter, Cassie.

Cassie was now, unbelievably, twenty-two years old and in law school at Cornell. After the Thanksgiving debacle reinforced the urgency of getting away from here, Misty asked Jess if she wanted to move to New York and split the rent on the perfect little duplex she and Jimmy'd found in the Bronx. Jess had jumped at the chance to fulfill a lifelong dream and be closer to her daughter.

I'm starting to think they're onto something.

What the hell was that supposed to mean?

Jess'd better not back out on this move. Misty could never afford the lease on a single income. Frowning, she turned off the light, locked up the shed, and trudged back to the house. Once she'd divested herself of dripping winter gear and delivered toilet paper to Jack, she returned to the recliner, cranked up the heat on the electric blanket, and answered Jessie's text.

Please tell me you're not buying into this end of the world bullshit, Juicy.

Misty wasn't the only one with an embarrassing high school nickname.

After a moment, three dots appeared. Jack emerged from the bathroom, hands intentionally damp to prove he'd washed them, and cuddled up next to her. As a pack of wild dogs destroyed the Old Man's Christmas turkey, Jessie's reply appeared.

What about Thanksgiving? What Jack & those kids said after the quake? It's all anyone talks about.

Then, after a few seconds, **What if it's NOT bullshit?**

Misty started typing an incredulous reply, but another text popped up before she'd finished the first word.

Come see me at the home tonight. I need to show you something.

Jess—who had no significant other, no parents, and a daughter seven hundred miles away—had volunteered for the night shift at Poplar Hill Nursing Home so her coworkers could be home with their families. She was like that, selfless to a fault. Saint Jessie of the Elderly and Infirm. Misty was the green-assed Grinch.

Um, thanks but no thanks. It's Christmas Eve!

Again, Jess's reply came in seconds.

Jack'll be in bed by 10. Just come by for an hour. It's important.

Important.

What was important was being here for her son on his first Christmas without his dad. All she wanted to do was put on Jimmy's Marine Corps sweatshirt, crawl in bed with Jack, and hold him tight in case the nightmares came back. She had no desire to spend even an hour of her Christmas in a nursing home that reeked of piss and isolation.

Jess was being weird, though. This wasn't like her at all. Maybe something was wrong. Maybe she'd lost a patient she was close to. Maybe Jess needed her.

One hour.

Uggghhh, FINE.

Instead of Jessie's typical effusive thank you, she sent one terse sentence in reply.

Be here by midnight.

And so, once her Santa Claus duties were done and Jack was sleeping soundly, Misty stuffed her pajama pants into salt-stained Uggs and snagged her dad's keys. She gave the '76 Dart a push to get it rolling, then coasted down the driveway. At the bottom of the hill, she fired up the engine and roared down the road blaring "Ain't Goin' Down" by Garth Brooks. Sneaking out and stealing her dad's car—1994 all over again.

As Jessie had instructed, she pulled the Dart around back and knocked on the door at the delivery entrance. A few frosty minutes later, the door opened and Jess appeared, sporting baby pink scrubs with a gingerbread man print.

Misty eyeballed the outfit and raised an eyebrow. "Fierce."

"Shut it, Boots," Jess said. Unlike Misty, whose mountain drawl had faded after twenty-plus years away from home, Jessie's accent was as strong as ever. "Get your ass in here. I'm freezin'."

Misty stepped inside, scraped snow off her boots on the welcome mat, and followed Jess down the silent hall to the nurse's station. Jess settled on a rolling stool and pushed a wheeled office chair her way.

"You working alone tonight?"

Jess shook her head, jingle bell earrings tinkling merrily. "Nope." She reached for a Buddy the Elf travel mug and took a few cautious sips of coffee. "Rhodie Mae's over in Memory Care tonight, and there's a night guard doin' rounds. Billy Collins," she said with a mischievous wink. "I'm sure you remember him."

Misty did, in fact, recall a rather disappointing three minutes in the back of a pickup, junior year. "Unfortunately." She looked down at Jimmy's stained sweatshirt and her baggy-assed flannel pants. "I'd rather not run into him at the moment, Juicy, so whatever it is you wanted to show me, let's get to it."

Jess's smile faded. She took a gulp of coffee and set the mug aside. Taking a deep breath, she stood and checked her watch. "Three minutes 'til midnight." She held out a hand to Misty. "Follow me."

Misty let Jess pull her to her feet, then followed her toward a dark hallway. Jesus H. Christ, it was creepy as *shit* in here, and the smell was just like she remembered from visiting Mamaw Moses. As they walked, motion-sensing lights flicked on, which made it feel a little less like the set of a horror movie, but only a little. Jess stopped in the middle of the hallway and grabbed Misty's hand.

"What are we—"

"Shhh!" Jessie looked from door to door. "We gotta listen," she whispered. "It's always only one of 'em, and it always happens at midnight."

Misty glanced up at the wall clock, watching the second hand tick toward the witching hour. The hand swung past midnight and continued on in a smooth arc.

"Jessie, for the love of—"

A quavering moan drifted from behind the door to their right. Jessie's eyes flicked toward Misty. Then she crossed the hall and opened the door. A nightlight provided enough illumination to avoid banging into the furniture, but the room was still veiled in shadows. She trailed Jess to the patient's bed. Once her eyes adjusted, Misty could make out a slight body that barely created a hill in the blankets, capped by a tuft of wispy white hair.

"Mrs. Pierce," Jessie said. "Are you all right?"

A gnarled hand emerged from the blanket, groping for the remote that controlled the incline on the bed. Jessie picked up the device and pressed it into the woman's hands. Swollen knuckles bulged as her fingers closed around it.

"I had a dream."

The old woman's voice was clear and strong, not what Misty had expected based on that warbling moan and her tiny body. She pushed a button on the remote, and the machinery whined as the upper third of the bed raised her to a mostly upright position. A different button lit the wall sconce next to her bed.

"I hope you don't mind, my friend stopped by for a Christmas visit." Jessie gestured toward her. "This is Misty."

The woman ignored her. She stared down at the remote, her lips moving in a soundless whisper.

Jessie perched on the edge of the bed and patted the back of a pale hand dotted with liver spots. "Is there anything I can—"

"I have to tell it," Mrs. Pierce said, looking up at Jessie. "I can't rest 'til I tell somebody. That's how it works."

Misty shivered. That's how *what* works?

The old lady leaned toward Jess. "A pale horse."

No.

No.

Not this bullshit. Not tonight.

"The dreams are all different, but they always start with a pale horse." Mrs. Pierce's tongue washed over withered lips. "The rider…" She squeezed her eyes shut and shook her head. "I can't see his face, but I know it's terrible. He's ridin' in from the east, and everywhere he passes, folks die."

Someone must've told her about what happened on Thanksgiving. Misty's eyes flicked to her best friend. Maybe it'd even been Jessie.

"He's ridin' through the streets of a city and… and bodies are pilin' up so fast there ain't nowhere to put 'em all." She opened her watery eyes, the faded blue of old denim, and stared at Misty. No… not at her—through her. "Trucks. They put 'em in trucks, stacked up like firewood."

When she didn't speak for a few moments, Jessie said, "That sounds awful, Mrs. P. I'm so sorry."

"There's a man walkin' the streets," she said. "A fine-lookin' man, but… but he's all covered in blood, and there's somethin' stickin' out of his chest. A piece of metal, looks like."

Her words hit Misty like a bucket of ice water. Jimmy… in the crash, he'd been…

Jessie must've told her about the accident. She must've set up this sick little charade. The icy shock blazed into white-hot rage. Misty shoved Jess so hard she almost fell on top of the old lady.

"If you don't want to go to New York, just fucking say so. But to do *this*? On Christmas?"

Jess sat up, reaching for her hand. "Misty, wait—"

She backed away. "Stay the hell away from me."

"I didn't know! Would you just—"

"The man sees me and says somethin'."

Misty turned and walked toward the door. Fuck this, and fuck Jess.

"He says, 'Tell her peek-a-boo says stay away.'"

She froze.

"What could that mean?" The old woman's voice was plaintive, confused. "It don't make no sense."

Misty crossed the room on wooden legs. "What did you just say?"

"I said it don't make—"

"Not that," she said, hearing the tremble in her voice. "What the man said."

"He said, 'Tell her peek-a-boo says stay away.'"

Peek-a-boo.

Misty fell to her knees. The unyielding hospital tile sent a jolt of pain from her kneecaps to the top of her skull. Jess slid off the bed and knelt next to her.

"Boots, what's goin' on?"

"The baby… the one I lost before Jackie…"

She and Jimmy had been married for five years and trying to get pregnant for three. When it finally happened, she'd been so happy. As tall as she was, Misty hadn't really shown until she was nearly six months along. Then one day, she woke up with a nice, round pregnant belly.

Peek-a-boo, Jimmy'd said, *I see you*.

He'd referred to their daughter as Peek-a-boo from that day

on. Nobody knew about that name—nobody but her and Jimmy.

And then when she was nearly eight months pregnant, she'd started bleeding and...

"That's what we called her," Misty said, her voice thick and hoarse. Tears streamed down her face. "Peek-a-boo."

Jess wrapped her arms around Misty and squeezed. "Oh, girl, I'm so sorry. I had no idea. I swear to God, I would never—"

A loud, ugly sob tore its way free deep inside Misty's chest, unleashing the flood of tears she hadn't shed since Jimmy died. She'd had to be strong for Jack, had to keep it together, but now, she couldn't help but fall apart. The breakdown was like a summer storm—violent, but brief. When the worst of it had passed, she let Jess help her to her feet. The old woman's eyes were locked on Misty's face.

"I'm real sorry, sugar, but I got to tell the end of the dream," she said. "I can't rest 'til I finish, and I'm so very tired."

Misty scrubbed her face with the sleeve of Jimmy's sweatshirt and nodded.

"After that man told me what to say, he pulled that metal thing out of his chest. It was like... like he was made of light." A child's smile lit up her wrinkled face. "He had *wings*."

EASTER

"Now this ain't my usual Easter sermon, y'understand." Though they were watching the livestreamed service on Dad's giant flatscreen TV, Reverend Sluss's eyes seemed to lock right on Misty. "But these ain't usual times, are they, friends?"

The dozen or so stubborn parishioners who'd braved the pandemic to attend in person produced a chorus of *No*'s.

"In the book of Revelations, chapter six, verse eight, John writes, 'And I looked, and behold a pale horse'—a pale horse, friends, just like our little 'uns foretold—'and his name that sat on him was Death, and Hell followed with him.'" He licked the tip of his index finger and began flipping through the Bible open in front of him. "Follow me now to the book of Acts, chapter two, verse seventeen." He traced his finger along the page, then looked up at the camera and said, "'And it shall come to pass in the last days, saith God, I will pour out of my Spirit upon all flesh: and your sons and your daughters shall prophesy, and your young men shall see visions, and your old men shall dream dreams.'"

He slammed the Bible shut and raised a triumphant fist. "We've seen it come to pass, ain't we? Revelations says the rider on the pale horse has the power to kill a fourth part of the Earth, and we're seein' those COVID numbers rise. Thousands dead, and—"

"Mama?"

Misty left her parents riveted by the Reverend's fiery words and walked to the small bedroom she and Jack shared. He was sitting on the floor with his Easter basket, surrounded by a drift of crumpled foil wrappers. "How much candy did you eat, baby?"

He looked up at her, revealing a face liberally smeared with chocolate and what looked like an oozing tendril of Cadbury's finest egg white. "Just a piece or two." He held up a shrink-wrapped plastic egg—one of those things all the kids were crazy about that contained a dozen cheap toys mired in putty. "Can you open this for me?"

She plopped down on the floor next to him and took the egg, turning it in her hands in hopes of finding a perforated seam. No luck. The freaking thing was hermetically sealed. She sighed and slid a fingernail under the edge of the wrapper.

"Is it real, Mom?"

Misty scowled at the egg, which plainly did not want to be opened. "What, the Easter bunny?"

Jack waved a dismissive hand. "That's kid stuff. The Easter bunny's not real. I mean, rabbits can't lay eggs…" His voice trailed off, and he looked up at her. "Right?"

She smiled. "Right."

"I meant God," he said. "Is God real?"

Well, *shit.*

"Mamaw told me what us kids said on Thanksgiving is coming true. And then that lady dreamed about Daddy, and I just… does that mean God is real and Dad's in Heaven?"

Maybe she shouldn't have told him about Mrs. Pierce's dream, but Jimmy was his father. Despite her morbid text message habit, before all this, Misty had believed dead meant extinguished—like blowing out a candle. But the dream showed her Jimmy was still watching over them. He still loved them. He was just somewhere else. Her son deserved to know that as much as she did.

"I don't know, Jackie." The plastic wrapper tore, and Misty slid the egg free and handed it to her son.

Her parents thought it was ridiculous that she'd been on the receiving end of not one but two prophetic revelations, and still lacked faith. Surely, by now, she could see the hand of God at work.

"I know there's something big and beautiful and good in this world," she said, "and I know it's looking out for us." She pulled Jack onto her lap and kissed the top of his blonde head. "When Daddy died, I was afraid he was gone forever, but now I know he's not." She shrugged. "Maybe Mamaw and Papaw are right. Maybe everything they believe is real. Or maybe those beliefs are like a language the big, beautiful something uses to talk to us. I can't say for sure, baby. I wish I could."

"Does this mean we'll get to see Daddy again one day?"

Misty closed her eyes, remembering the poem Jimmy's sister had read at his funeral. *Do not stand at my grave and weep. I am not there. I do not sleep. I am the thousand winds that blow. I am the diamond glints on snow...*

"I think it means we've never stopped seeing him." She looked down at Jack, at his big green eyes—so like his father's. "Daddy's always here. We just have to look with our eyes closed."

Jack squeezed his eyes shut. "I think I see him, Mama," he whispered.

Misty rested her chin on his head. She might not know if she believed in God, but she believed in Jimmy. She believed in Peek-a-boo. And she believed in undying love.

That was more than enough.

SLOW BEGINNING
By Anne Johnston

This is a time of fast changes and slow beginnings.

The long slow mulling of things to come and

How or where or when to grow.

Seeds of brilliant flowering asleep under autumnal drift.

The joyous starts of violent births and

Revivals in hidden caverns, building pressure far below.

This is a time of turmoil and stasis.

The deep desiring for something normal and

Escape from routine awaiting realization.

A BRAND NEW WORLD
By Marília Bonelli

THE MONSTERS ARE EVERYWHERE.

I can see them roaming the barren streets every once in a while. The streets have never been this empty before. It's been weeks since I've seen an actual human out there.

Now, except for a few small critters under the cover of darkness, the world stands still.

As for when it happened…

It's as if one day, the world turned upside down. It's a scary thought that the "normal" you are so used to could vanish just like that.

Thankfully, I am not alone. Well, not usually.

I don't think I could bear it if I didn't have my one companion. She left this morning in search of food, venturing out into the unknown while I remain safely hidden away.

Even on this side of the barrier, I'm afraid.

My whole body tingles when I watch them go by. They disguise themselves as humans, but even from afar, the difference is obvious. They have the size and most of the movement down, but those large waiting mouths, either black or white—that's not something they can hide. They can't fool me.

The monsters see me sometimes. At least I'm safe inside my fortress. I know they cannot reach me here.

It is not an ideal existence, being trapped in a prison—even one with no bars.

I've almost forgotten what it was like before. The feel of the sun on my face during those early quiet mornings my companion and I spent together, the gentle breeze that accompanied nightfall. I miss those simple things.

In my most desperate hours, I've thought about escaping. I went as far as trying, but my companion's panicked shrieks and the monsters that lurked outside struck such fear in me that my feet never even touched the grass.

I do not wish to see what horrors lie beyond the empty streets.

Maybe the monsters are devouring every unsuspecting creature they run across—is that why everyone is suddenly gone? And what of the monsters themselves? Will they devour each other in the end until nothing remains but the squirrels? Or will they devour even the squirrels?

The darkening skies, ominous as they are, seem to mock me. Shadows rise from every corner of our fortress, stressing that I am still alone.

Why hasn't she returned? It'll be dark soon. Her eyesight isn't that good in the dark.

I've never worried about her safety before, but these are not normal circumstances.

A world filled with monsters is *not* normal!

Normal.

Will my life ever be normal again? Will the world?

The familiar sound of footsteps right outside the door makes my heart beat a little faster. I would know those sounds in my sleep.

Finally!

My companion has returned. My heart beats merrily in my chest as I run to greet her. But as quickly as relief came, terror takes its place. I am deceived for a moment, but then it turns its head, and its narrowed gaze suddenly locks onto mine. Instead of my beloved companion, a monster stands at the entrance. The dark gaping mouth is ready and waiting.

I skid on the floor, my legs trying to change course without stopping their movement as I turn and run.

I mustn't let it catch me!

I don't want to be eaten by a monster.

Hide! A place to hide!

I run into the bedroom, my eyes wide as they adjust to the darkness. I scramble into the closet, tucking myself into the shadows. I remain as still as I can; even my breathing is soundless. I focus all of my attention on the surrounding silence. For a moment, I hear nothing but distant rustling as the monster moves around near the entrance. It is apparently in no hurry to find me. I can't relax, though, not when it starts moving further away from the door.

The footsteps, deceptively similar to my companion's, come increasingly closer. The light in the room suddenly comes on, a slit of brightness breaching my hiding place and blinding me before I can blink.

Movement draws nearer. Right in front of the closet, it stops.

The monster emits a horrible, astringent odor. It is even hard to breathe.

I struggle not to make a sound.

"Mavros?" a familiar voice calls out.

How has the monster stolen my companion's voice?

Panic glues me in place. It grows harder and harder to breathe through the stench.

Finally, the monster moves away, a merciful respite.

I start when the sound of falling water coming from the bathroom breaks through the terrible silence.

Then comes the sound of crashing things and a short cry of pain.

What is going on? Is there a fight? But who's in there with the monster? Have I been so distracted by the creature that I didn't hear another's footsteps?

Please don't let it be another monster.

There are no other smells than the lingering pungent odor and the pervasive smell of my companion—this is her closet, after all.

After what feels like an eternity, silence falls again. My dread intensifies with every approaching footstep as the creature returns to my hiding place. It is too late to run away now. Fighting is my only chance. I prepare to attack.

The door flies open and, as I am about to pounce, a surprised gasp stops me cold.

It isn't the monster…

My companion is alive!

Where's the monster? Has it been defeated?

I rush toward the bathroom, stopping as I reach the threshold. If the monster is still in there—if it still lives—will I be able to finish the job?

Staying close to the ground, I sneak in, stealthy, not a sound beneath my feet.

Even with the added smells that tried to hide my companion's scent, the stench of the monster is easy to find.

It is dead now. Nothing but the outer layers remain. I sniff at the pile lying at the edge of a water puddle, all that is left of the monster. The gaping blackness of its mouth still awaits atop the heap, inert, but no less scary. Four dark tendrils lifelessly reach out along the tiled floor.

I draw nearer, ready to strike at the smallest sign of movement. There is none. Its eyes are nowhere to be seen, and there is no breath or motion.

Apparently, the monster had the same weakness I do, but it was unexpectedly fragile. Just one bath destroyed it. I shudder, thankful that my companion was able to kill it after the battle.

Something touches my back. I jump up and whirl around, landing in the puddle I'd just been observing.

I back up quickly as my companion reaches down and grabs the dark remnants of the monster's mouth. "Oh, there's my mask."

She stares down at me with a smile. "Aw, kitty, did I scare you? Come on, I'll give you some food. You want food?"

Despite the droplets of water falling on my face from her long, wet fur, I trail happily after her. The monster has been defeated by my brave companion using the evil rainmaker she calls shower.

Why shouldn't we enjoy a feast? The monsters are everywhere, but they are all outside.

JUST POTATOES
By Gabrielle Gold

WHEN HE STARTED WINTER break, Sam was not expecting company on Christmas. But here he was, walking down 21st Street with Emily Huang, watching snowflakes cling to her hair. They were not holding hands, though. He wasn't ready for that.

"…my aunt brought me there, and now it's a staple of mine. I'm pretty sure you'll like it." Emily didn't talk with her hands like his family did. But she didn't need to. Her dimpled smile was enough.

"It's Chinese food. How bad could it be?" Laughing, Sam tried to pay attention as she launched into a rambling response about how different the cuisine was between provinces. It wasn't a lack of interest on his part. She was just even cuter in person than online. Distractingly so.

He had only known her from the Ultimate Frisbee club in high school, but OkCupid paired her with him three times in the past year. After a chance encounter on Tuesday at Starbucks, he decided it was fate.

"…the northeast part of the country. They use ingredients you probably wouldn't expect." Emily raised her eyebrows. "When I say 'lamb stew,' do you think China?"

"I think Ireland." He glanced at both street corners. "Shouldn't it be around here somewhere?"

"It's on the other side. Let's cross." Once she pointed it out, he could easily spot the sign reading *Manchurian Wok* in neon green half-script. The window below flashed OPEN like a signal beacon while block lettering on the door proclaimed *We Do Takeout!*

It all screamed "generic Chinese place."

"Right." Adjusting his glasses, Sam let her take the lead.

Inside, the combined aroma of chilies and garlic wafted towards them. White linen covered the tables, but everything else seemed cheap. The metal chairs were another callback to high school. At least a poster of colorful pottery and cookware brightened the space.

There weren't many customers. An Asian couple was a promising sign, but not so much the older white women. One of the ladies looked familiar. Maybe he had seen her at synagogue some year, back when he still bothered.

A man behind the counter brought menus and two plastic tumblers of ice water to their table before leaving them to their own devices.

"Interesting stuff." Sam eyed the more authentic-looking section. "There's your lamb stew. I'll pass on the beef intestines. Hmm…wait, there are potatoes in Chinese food?"

"What are you looking at?" Emily's bangs draped in her face

as she leaned forward to read the upside-down options. "Oh! Cumin potato. I love that dish. It's dry-fried."

"Hold up." He squinted at her. "I know fried potatoes. My mom just made latkes for Hanukkah. There's no way this will compare."

"Chinese food *absolutely* knows fried potatoes." She sat back as if he had slandered her grandmother. "Now you have to get them. They're so good."

"Come on. Nothing beats homemade. Her recipe's been in our family for decades." Realizing he was using the tone he usually reserved for his nine-year-old cousin, he stopped.

The waiter returned. "Do you know what you would like?"

"I want the Dì Sān Xiān." Emily grabbed both menus and handed them over. "He wants cumin potato."

Before he could protest, the waiter disappeared into the kitchen. Sam drummed his fingers on the tabletop.

Emily stared at her paper placemat for too long before slowly meeting his eyes. "I thought you liked trying new things."

"I do." He glanced sideways. "Are you proud of your culture? Other than the food, I mean."

"Sure, I am. Why?"

"I guess I want something to be loyal to." His restless fingers came to a halt. "Even if it's just Jewish potatoes."

"Oh." She folded in the corners of her napkin. "Can't we share them?"

Sam decided not to mention that Hanukkah memorialized an ancient war over national identity. "I wish it were that simple."

When the waiter arrived with two steaming heaps of food, he

knew which one was his.

"Whoa." Sam inhaled. The thick, golden potato slices wore beautiful coats of spices. "Ok, that looks amazing."

"Try one." Her outstretched hand stopped an inch from his plate. "May I? We can swap."

Grateful he had been schooled in the use of chopsticks, Sam selected a chunk of eggplant from her dish and nodded. Then he dug in. "Holy crap, these are great."

"Told you." She beamed.

He savored a crispy piece. "I concede. China knows fried potatoes."

"I'm sure they're nothing like your mom's."

Holding up a slice, he considered it for a moment. "No. They're awesome in a different way."

By the time they left the restaurant, they were holding hands.

AN ENDURING LOVE
By Marília Bonelli

WITH THE FLIP OF a switch, dozens of small lights came to life along the pathway, filling Fynn's eyes with as many stars as the sky.

Estelle always loved stars. Well, with a name like that, how could she not?

In school, she would spend hours drawing endless starry nights in the corners of her notebooks. Even his hand, that soft spot between his index finger and his thumb, would become a canvas for her constellations. Fynn unclenched his fists, rubbing that spot as if some trace of ink remained from years ago.

Maybe it was because he'd finally returned after four years of college—practically another dimension—but those memories he'd filed away flooded his mind the moment he set foot in this over-decorated ode to Christmas he'd once called home.

His gaze wandered along the peeling paint at the edge of the gazebo before rising above the trees, searching for lights from his house. His bedroom, unchanged after all these years, still held the ghosts of their study sessions—meetings that quickly and inevitably derailed into a different kind of session. Traces of her were everywhere. He'd even found one of her scrunchies in a desk drawer—purple with silver stars.

Like a sudden wave in a tranquil pool, Estelle had overwhelmed his senses. It wasn't just his room, either. The entire town was filled with echoes of love and laughter. The path they walked home from school, the spot by the lake where they hid from the world, even the sidewalk where they'd shared their first kiss in front of an amused salesperson.

His life was inextricably linked to Estelle. He couldn't fathom how he'd managed to be apart from her for so long.

Fynn turned the lights off. It wasn't time yet. The main event wasn't supposed to happen until midnight. Making sure nothing else spilled out of his pocket, he pulled out his cell phone, blinking when the screen was a bit too bright.

Three messages, none of them from her. But that was to be expected.

He opened the messages, all from his cousin Kate, each five minutes apart.

Can we leave yet?

I'm having trouble stalling. Your future wife *fingers crossed* is getting angry.

Apparently, I'm not good enough company. :(She's threatening to go home since you stood her up.

Midnight was fast approaching, but most everything was ready. He was typing a message to Kate to let her know he was waiting on the flowers when Gary came jogging up the darkened path carrying a bouquet of lilies. He huffed and puffed as if ready to blow some poor pig's house down.

"You might wanna start thinking about exercising more."

"I get enough exercise chasing my four-year-old."

Gary had gotten married right out of high school. Even Kate tied the knot last year. Out of their small group of friends, he was the only one left unwed.

"Far be it from me to question you, but are you sure your girl likes these flowers?" Gary asked, clumsily trying to straighten the lilies before handing over. "Don't girls usually prefer roses? At least my wife does."

"I'm not sure what her favorite flower is." He'd picked these because they reminded him of stars.

Gary raised his hands up in surrender. "Hey, it's your neck."

"Can you let Kate know I'm ready for her?" Fynn fussed with the flowers, rearranging them until he was satisfied.

"Please bring over the unsuspecting prey—I mean, the bride to be," Gary read aloud as he typed. He slid his phone into his pocket and gave Fynn an enthusiastic thumbs up. "Do you need anything else?"

"Thanks, man. I think I'm good." Despite his reply, a touch of cold crept into his body, running from the top of his head to the tip of his toes.

Gary left through the other side of the gazebo, leaving Fynn alone to wait.

He stuffed his hands into his pockets. His right hand edged

away when it touched the small velvety box. His left clutched the folded letter, already crumpled and damp with sweat.

Fynn released it, stifling the urge to look once again at the familiar loops of Estelle's handwriting.

This was it, wasn't it? The last choice. The last chance to turn back. But what would he even turn toward?

He stroked one of the soft petals with his fingertips, careful not to disturb the arrangement. Maybe he should have gotten a vase or something. Nah, she'd love it either way.

The flowers sat beautifully on the small table in the center of the gazebo. Even in the dim light, the white petals were a bright contrast against the blue tablecloth. It was only a shade darker than Estelle's eyes.

Fynn drew a deep breath of chilly midnight air. Cold sweat ran down his back. He tried to think of the words he wanted to say, but memories of Estelle's smile overshadowed everything else.

He should have written down what he wanted to say, should have planned better. But he hadn't had his thoughts straight since that morning. His left hand stopped halfway to his pocket. He didn't dare continue.

The night felt a little darker than before. Silence stretched for several minutes, not even murmurs from the outside world breached the barrier of surrounding trees. This had also been one of their favorite spots, where they could lose themselves in each other's kisses, interrupted only by wayward dogs and their frantic owners.

Footsteps sounded on the stone path, an echo of the past

suddenly come to life. Familiar voices intruded next.

"Kate, why are we—"

Fumbling for the switch, Fynn turned on the lights, temporarily stunning the two girls.

He took a sharp, deep breath. Then he stepped out of the shadows.

Kate gave the couple a furtive smile, flashing two thumbs up as she retreated.

"Fynn? What's going on?" Her gaze followed the lights, found him. Nervous hands clutched at the hem of her dress. She hadn't taken another step. The trace of a smile wavered on her lips.

Fynn could tell she was teetering on the edge of excitement, perhaps unwilling to reveal her expectations in case she was wrong.

Still unable to think of the right words, he shoved his sweaty hands in his pockets as he walked over to her.

His right hand fingered the soft little box.

His left hand gripped the folded letter.

The right hand emerged with the box, but still the left wouldn't—*couldn't*—let go.

His girlfriend was holding her breath now, her eyes locked on the box with unbridled anticipation. Fynn flipped it open, revealing the delicate ring. Light reflected onto the small stones, laid out perfectly to form a star at its center.

Her bright green eyes tearfully gazed up at him. She was so silly, laughing and crying at the same time like that. He was right, she'd love it regardless of the shape.

His left hand released the goodbye letter he'd gotten from his one true star that morning and took the crying girl's hand in his.

"Aubrey Jean Lamar, will you marry me?"

THIS HOUSE RECALLS YOU

By J. Levesque

This house recalls you.

It stands as though you live here still,

isolated from the concrete city

by a veil of branches burdened with green summer rain.

I sit inside my car and watch long stains appear

as gutters flood and wash its cedar face.

We captured sunlight in that stained-glass door,

burned a lamp behind it in the hall.

But now, it's dark.

I run through mud-splashed weeds and use the realtor's key.

My image flickers in the shadowed glass.

After years alone, you wouldn't know me.

Rain hammers at the roofing tin. It brings back other times

we heard that sound.

Inside, I flick the light switch. Nothing happens

so, I haunt the hall until my eyes accept

this clouded afternoon

then wander through these rooms.

They look the same.

Plank floors and ceilings held apart

by massive, upright beams

still seem solid, strong.

This wooden staircase rises from the open living space

to shuttered bedrooms.

Fireplaces stand in every one, cold now,

ashes scraped away and buried.

The furniture is gone.

Behind another door, the clawed tub stands alone

on hand-glazed tiles,

remembering how we felt in its embrace.

Upstairs, the rain is closer.

I stay awhile and stare through antique panes.

§

Outside again, I shut the door. Its handle

and the useless switch

are all I've touched.

Live oaks reach for one another across the twisted drive.

From this angle, I can see

they never meet.

THE RUINS
By Autumn Shah

THE TRIP HAD BEEN my idea. The location, his.

As the house seemed more and more stagnant, and I wanted to leave it less and less, I realized I must, or else I'd be trapped, forever roaming rooms no longer used.

I had pictured the hills and mountains, the opulence of Austria or Switzerland. When Ted declared he wanted to go somewhere warm and exotic I suggested Majorca, a common holiday spot for us Britons and a place with which we were familiar. But no, he was imagining the trip of a lifetime, prized photographs he could share with his friends on the slide projector.

"I've dreamed of going to India ever since I read *A Passage to India*, in my sixth form," he told me. "I must have been fifteen at the time."

That was news to me. I'd never heard the word *India* pass through his lips. But no matter, I didn't know enough about India to be troubled by his choice. So, I read *The Raj Quartet* series and *The Far Pavilions*, which had just come out. Ted read the guidebooks, watched the travel programs, and talked incessantly with the travel agent down the lane.

I wasn't worried about not being able to drink the water or eat fresh fruit; we'd been to Algeria and Morocco. Making do with coffee and alcohol and exploring markets for well-cooked, local delicacies was nothing new to us. We could speak barely a word of Spanish when we went on holiday to Madrid. We gave it a good go, using our phrasebook any chance we got. We had even taken little Marcus with us then, only four years old at the time.

Ted found another couple, his colleague Andrew, who taught in the linguistics department, and his wife Doris, who had visited India the year before. He invited them for dinner so he could barrage them with questions. They were a charming couple, willing to ignore the sadness evident in the dusty table centerpiece made of dried larkspur, ragged lady, and yarrow grown in the front garden. Could they sense the absence of a bike thrown down in the driveway, or the Gray-Nicolls cricket bat that once rested against the wall beside the front door? I shove such thoughts aside and muster a smile for our guests.

Andrew and Doris had thoroughly enjoyed their trip to India. I admit, their enthusiasm sparked my own excitement. We used to love to travel.

"Can't trust most of those Indians though," Andrew said as we helped them into their coats.

"Whatever do you mean?" I asked, a bit put off.

"It's a poor country, isn't it? Everyone's corrupt. You have to be careful. You just have to watch yourself."

We'd been warned similarly regarding thieves in Spain and Italy, but nothing untoward had happened.

"It's true, Peg," Doris whispered confidentially as she buttoned up her lavender pea-coat. "I caught several young native boys peeping into our room. Apparently, one of them was making money by selling space in front of the tiniest hole!" She shuddered.

"And a friend told us a horrific story about her trip," Doris continued, raising her voice over our husbands' conversation. "A tour guide, or someone posing as a tour guide, took her and her husband to some out-of-the-way temple in the south of India. Got them there, held them at knife-point, snipped the money belt from the husband's waist, and left them in the jungle. But not before knocking the husband out cold, mind you. The poor chap tried to get the passports out before handing over the belt. Can you imagine?" Her hand fluttered to her chest. "Fortunately, she was carrying the passports in an inside pocket of her vest!"

"So, what happened?"

"Thank goodness for hippies! A group came through and took them to a village where they arranged for a driver to take them back to the city."

"Oh my," I breathed.

"Well, never mind. There are plenty of good stories about India. But it's always the bad ones you remember, isn't it?" Ted said.

When we exit the airport in Kota, it is teeming with people.

"Keep the camera bags close, pet," Ted tells me. "Thieves hang about outside these airports."

I hide his two precious camera bags against my side, under my satchel.

The following two days we explore the city and acclimate to the time change. The morning air is crisp, yet after a few short hours, it turns blistering: though a dry heat that we British adore. My sleeveless cotton dress reaches my ankles. Over that I wear a three-quarter-sleeved linen shift and a hat that I am never without while under a savage sun.

We walk out of our hotel, the former palace of a maharaja. We see the usual men on the street lean against their cars and rickshaws, spitting tobacco, smoking, and gabbing loudly. This is our third morning, but we must still look ripe for the picking, for a man in a suit saunters across the road towards us. He twirls a heroic moustache with one hand while the other rests in the pocket of his gabardine slacks. He looks a bit of a rake with his shirtfront open. His eyes are a strange color, more green than the expected brown, and his eyebrows slant a bit too salaciously above his long lashes. I move closer to Ted.

"Need driver somewhere, sir? In the city or out we will go." He brandishes a hand across the street, gesturing to a car we can't pick out amidst the jumble.

"No, actually," Ted replies. "We have a driver scheduled."

We look about for signs of a driver awaiting us.

The man looks down at the guidebook Ted holds.

"This is where you are wanting?"

Ted holds the dog-eared page open and attempts to pronounce the site. "Yes. Chit-or-gar."

"Yes, yes, outside city. Chittorgarh. You want to see the fort, isn't it?"

"Yes, that's it."

"Come, come. I have nice car. Air and smooth riding. I give you good price."

I am surprised, and sorely tempted by the notion of air conditioning after the last two days touring in oven-like heat. "Thank you, but we have a driver already."

"You need more than driver, madam. Where you want to go, you need guide too. I am taking persons there all the time. It is big place, and you need guide *and* driver."

Ted shoos him away as we continue to scan the area for the maroon Ambassador we were told to look for.

"It looks like they are not here, sir, madam. Happens all the time."

"We'll give a minute or so, then I say we go on with this chap," Ted says to me.

It shouldn't matter, but I want that maroon car to appear. It's what was scheduled, what was planned. We wait a few minutes, looking up and down the bustling road, and when it doesn't appear, Ted waves to the man, a slight gesture of his raised hand as we head in their direction. "Sir, yes," the man says. "You will not be regretting."

The driver turns towards his car, making sure we follow. Shouldn't we check out his "nice car"? Shouldn't we ask what his "good price" is? As we approach, my anxiety surges when a second man hops off the hood of a dirty white Ambassador, flicking his cigarette into the road in the same movement. This shorter, pot-bellied man opens the driver's side and gets in. I am about to voice my concerns to Ted, but the Brylcreem-glossed fellow slinks to the other side of the car, proffering the door as if it were the Queen's carriage. The combination of pushiness and deference we have encountered in Indians is confusing and makes me wary. I climb into the faded red leather interior.

I don't know if the driver also speaks English, so I whisper to Ted, "Don't you think we should talk about this first? How much are they going to charge us for both of them?" I don't mention the bad vibes I have about our guide and my qualms about there being a duo.

He pats my arm. "Don't worry about money, darling. We're on holiday."

The "guide" speaks under his breath to the driver, and the driver starts the car. Why whisper when we can't understand the language? Our ignorance of the native language has not bothered me before. But it does now.

It is only minutes before we are embroiled in the frenzied traffic of India. The "air" the guide referred to is an oscillating fan attached to the dashboard with a cord that snakes underneath. Each time it turns past me, a wisp of hair clings to my glossed lips.

I look out the window past the cars, motorbikes, bicycles, camel carts, and pedestrians sharing the road. I imagine myself out of this car and walking across the hills in the distance. Far from the smell of cheap cologne and leather-cleaning oil. Far from Ted and his guileless enthusiasm to make this trip a success, to make me forget what I still, six years on, am not ready to forget.

"I'm so eager, aren't you, Margaret?" He practically bounces in his seat. "I think this will be the place where we can truly experience India and feel its history running through our veins. I want to stand on the very soil where battle lines were drawn up, where heroes were made, and plots were whispered in the isolated aerie of the towers."

"Ted, please," I say, softening some. "You were always the romantic."

Suddenly the car jerks to a stop that throws us forward and back again. At the same moment, there is a crunch of metal, and brakes screech as cars around us swerve and stop. The guide scolds the driver and wallops him across the head. I look at Ted in astonishment. But Ted is busy watching out the window, trying to discern what's going on.

"One moment please, sirs," our guide says.

The two men exit the car and walk over to a rusting blue Premier our car has butted. A woman climbs out from the passenger side and screeches a storm at anyone who will listen while her twig-like husband tries to calm her. Our guide points to a metal bumper on the road and the driver picks it up and hands it to the husband as the wife squawks on.

Our guide strides to the side of the road to confront an unkempt-looking man pulling his bike up from the pavement. The car ahead of us must have barely missed him. Our guide swats the cyclist across the head, and Ted takes hold of my hand. The men begin yelling at each other but go quiet again. The man who had been swiped off his bike puts his hands together and looks to be almost bowing to our guide. The husband from the car we rear-ended joins them, along with the driver, while traffic moves on around us, having lost interest.

It is only then that I notice two children, a teenage girl and a young boy, staring at us out the back window of the bumper-less car. The boy appears to be the same age my Marcus will now always be. He has the same unnerving, incisive look in his eyes that makes my breath catch.

"Maybe we should get out," I say. "Check to make sure everything is alright."

"No. I'm sure our men can take care of it. They seem to know what they're doing," Ted responds.

His words cause my stomach to writhe. This is the way he's always been. When Marcus went missing, I wanted action, answers. Ted, polite to a fault, accepted that the police services and detectives were doing all they could. Besieged by his own anguish, he paced the police station waiting for them to find answers. Meanwhile, I walked the city streets and the country lanes searching for my son. For me, anger and impatience fought for room with grief, even as we later buried him.

The four men conclude their dialogue with affable smiles and sideways glances at us. The driver pats the husband's shoulder and guides him back to his own car. As far as I can tell, they haven't exchanged cards or information, and this strikes me as odd.

"Sorry about that madam," our guide says, as they both climb back into the car. "Small thing. Happens all the time here, yes?" He rests his arm over the top of the bench seat.

As we start off again, Ted settles back in his seat. We drive out of the city and pass barren plains, scruffy patches of brush, and what looks like desolate farmland. How do people survive on this land? They must be hardy people. My mind wanders, not in the direction of the evocative landscape, but back to what just transpired. What if the whole thing had been staged? What if it had been a rendezvous point, to let the man on the bicycle know they had picked up fare—or rather, victims? Perhaps the bicyclist made a phone call, relaying information to their cronies about where they were taking us, where they should meet up. What if the "accident" had allowed them to tie up their plans?

I fight against my ruminations, telling myself I am foolish, dreaming up the stuff of novels. But I know better than most that these things happen. It's the oblivious who fall victim. I used to be one of them. I cling to this kind of karmic thinking to soothe myself. If I imagine it and recognize the possibility, perhaps it *won't* happen merely because I know it can.

We drive up a winding precipice, the tangled ruins of the fort high above. From afar, it reminds me of our more dilapidated castles in England. The crenellated turrets and enduring walls. The crawling moss and piles of rubble. I had looked forward to sensing the history of this place, like Ted, feeling that vibration that passes through a person that can't be felt in modernized or rebuilt ancient sites, its honest decrepitude, but I find myself weaving all sorts of gruesome scenarios based on stories from friends, and friends of friends, and all those novels I read before coming, as well as my own macabre imagery. The set jaw of our guide as he walloped the cyclist over the head. I try to picture our guide and driver with families, small children on their laps, climbing on their backs, any image to soften them in my mind. But all this does is force me to think how much more desperate having a family can make a person.

A sizable town is nestled within Ram Pol, one of seven gates that surround Chittorgarh. The stones that make it up are smoothed, large squares, heavy, but with delicate engravings of elephants, or buffalo; it's hard to tell at the speed we drive by. We continue past a white-washed temple that Ted cranes his neck to examine. The car putters upward and our guide points out the two cenotaphs of warriors who fought in the last battle of Chittorgarh in the sixteenth century.

"Say, could we stop and have a look around here?" Ted asks.

"Sir, it is best that we go to the top a ways and enjoy the early morning, and then come down. Soon, the sun will be too much and more people will come, and they will go to top first and you will not be enjoying to the fullest. Yes?"

"Quite right, then," Ted says.

They want to get us up there alone. My eyes dart to look out the back window. From our vantage point, I can see for miles. I see villagers, as small as mice, squatting next to their wares, riding bikes, walking purposefully with loads balanced upon their heads. I am relieved no one is trailing us, unless there is another route up I can't see. At the same time, I am chilled by the fact that there are no other vehicles in sight.

"I want to go back to the hotel," I say. The words burst from my lips of their own accord.

The driver and guide cease their chatter with one another. The guide looks back at us.

"Whatever for?" Ted asks. He looks at me as if I am mad. "Are you feeling alright, Peg?"

"I don't know. I'm not feeling myself."

"Maybe it's the drive. We're almost there now."

I'm very aware of the men up front listening. "Yes, you might be right. I'll be right as rain once we're out and about."

Ted gives me a small smile and a nod, likely grateful I'm being a good sport.

I imagine myself taking him by the lapels of his gingham shirt, tears in my eyes. Telling him we must run *now*. But I can't justify the action on a *bad feeling*. As the car slows to a crawl through yet another gate, I picture us opening the doors and throwing ourselves out. We'll stumble down the embankment as quickly as we can and hide in the sparse forest that skirts the path until a villager takes pity on us or more tourists arrive.

I feel better now that I have a plan of escape, but it also makes me aware of my own foolishness. These men have probably taken hundreds of people to visit the fort and shown them historical wonders, given them secret histories the guidebooks don't share. They are probably honest men working for a living, and I am being ridiculous and paranoid and wasting this opportunity. My eyes catch the driver's in the rearview mirror and I quickly look away, then back again, my hands fluttering in my lap.

"I'm Peg," I say, my voice high and warbly. "And this is Ted."

The guide turns a bit in his seat. "Good, good. I am Dilip. He is Rajesh."

"Nice to meet you." I nod, and prattle on. "We only just arrived a couple of days ago. There is so much to see, we hardly knew where to start."

"India is full of wonders," Dilip says. "But you made good choice to come here."

"Crikey," Ted says, looking up from his guidebook, and rescuing me from further jittery blabbering. "I'm just reading here that this entire fort area spans more than three miles."

"Yes, this is right," Dilip confirms. "Within, are many Rajput palaces, monuments, and numerous temples, as well as the fort itself. *Too much* to see," he says, flicking his hand off his forehead for emphasis.

If I give myself a moment, perhaps I *can* feel the history here, the women who lived behind the closed walls, the security they felt living behind seven gates, and walls several feet thick, the confidence, then the slowly creeping fear of being besieged. They were fooled into thinking they were safe. But all it takes is one chink in their defense and the whole thing tumbles down.

Nervous dread roils in the pit of my stomach, and I feel again the overwhelming urge to get us out. My heart pounds, my breath catches somewhere between my chest and my throat. I grip the door handle and force myself to breathe, evenly, counting between exhales. I am certain every gate we pass through takes us further toward our doom.

Ted looks at me with concern, but he babbles on about a tower and a maharaja and his words are muffled by the roaring in my ears. I try to concentrate. I force a smile. Sometimes I can trick myself into being okay if I just force my lips to curl upward.

"Darling, you're perspiring. Should I have the driver turn the fan on you?"

"Yes, that might help."

Ted signals for them to turn the fan. Dilip presses down the knob and the head of the fan stays trained on me. He goes back to looking out the window, twisting and twirling that moustache with his slender fingers.

Ted's gaze lingers on me a little too long, it seems he might say something, like he *wants* to say something. But he turns away. This is where we've ended up. Unable to talk about that thing that both connects us and tears us apart. When my silent tears materialize during dinner, Ted studies the backs of his hands. When I clutch the copy of *The Borrowers* that Marcus never got to finish, the very book that had been in the basket of his bike, found on the street pointed toward home, Ted smiles fondly. I know he is grieving. What I don't know is how he endures it.

Rajesh stops the car in a gravelly patch where tumbled boulders surround a decrepit tower that seems determined to maintain its imposing presence. I don't want to get out of the car, but I do. I climb out from the backseat and straighten the creases in my dress while Ted grabs the camera bag. Myriad structures in various stages of disintegration dot the area. Balconies, fallen walls, stairways that quit midair. Rajesh and Dilip flank us. I can't concentrate on the words coming from Dilip's lips. I need to be alert. I need to be one step ahead.

I think of my Marcus. Plucked off his bike. Taken, and then murdered. I fight continually against the image of his broken body, found three days later in a narrow field of cow parsley along a country road. Did the man who took him stalk him first? Did Marcus try to escape? Did he fight at all? The terror and confusion Marcus must have felt. Did he scream for me? Where was I at that moment? I wasn't there for him, he was all alone, no one answering his screams.

A piercing, inhuman shriek erupts from the quiet. I jump and clutch the camera bag to my chest. Ted's fingers claw at my arm. Rajesh points up to a black-faced monkey grinning down at us with bared teeth. Several langurs lounge on the wall, watching us fixedly.

"Must watch for the monkeys," Dilip says. "They will steal your pocketbook or your camera. They will even jump on the lady's pretty blonde hairs." He laughs, and the driver joins in. Ted's face is red, but he chuckles politely.

The men guide us along twisting paths and confusing corners that lead to the walls of the fort. Rajesh stays a few feet behind when we walk on. He smokes a cigarette, pretending boredom, yet his eyes follow our every step.

We come upon an intact part of the main wall. It must be at least ten feet high with intimidating sawtooth crenellations along the top. The jagged, stacked stones are cool to the touch, still retaining the cool of the night. We walk through a crumbling archway that leads to the steep, rocky slope on the other side. I take note of the naked trees far below reaching out to each other, boulders blanketed by parched moss and grasses.

This is it then. Any second now they're going to shove us off this plateau and steal from our broken bodies. Or they'll muscle us first, take what they want, and then push us to our deaths.

I wait for a shift in their movements, something that tells me they are closing in. When it doesn't come, I want to confront them, get it over with, but they seem not concerned with us at all. Rajesh appears to be enjoying the view himself, his mind somewhere else. While Dilip is mesmerized by the lit cigarette between his fingers.

When Ted is satisfied we walk back through the archway, back into the fort complex, unharmed. I am not mollified. They didn't use that opportunity. They have a better plan then.

We drive a brief way with the windows down, though no air seems to pass through at all.

"There are many different ways to see the wonders of this place. There is no order but that which you create from the story you want to tell," the tour guide says eloquently. "We will walk now the ruins of the Khumba Palace."

Ted read to me on the plane about Khumba Palace. It was built by the Rajput dynasty in the eighth century but kept its name from the king who renovated it in the fifteenth. It's the largest structure within these gates, and from there we can look down on the whole breathtaking complex.

It is much ruined with collapsed walls and fallen debris, but there are still a great many places to walk about. I try to telepathically send a warning to Ted, but instead he follows the guide, leading me in and out of corridors and chambers, past dreamy pavilions and more stairways leading to nowhere. The crumbling walls are burdened with secrets. I feel I am being watched from the multitude of windows and towers that look down on us.

Dilip leads us down some steps, and with all the drama he can muster, tells us the story of Rani Padmini, the wife of King Rawal Ratan Singh, and a neighboring sultan, Alauddin Khilji. How the sultan fell mad with love after he saw her face reflected in a mirror within her palace, down the hill from us, how he fought his way into the fort to claim her as his own. Here, the guide's voice grows somber.

"It was in this courtyard, where we are standing, that the queen and the women and children had *great* fire lighted and threw themselves into this fire. This is including the brave Rana Padmini herself. They committed the massed suicide rather than face the dishonor at the hands of the enemy coming through the gates." He seems mesmerized by his own story, one he must have revised and recited many times.

"Over seven hundred ladies and children…" his voice trails off as he whispers, casting sidelong glances about him. As if he too is being watched.

"Maybe it is best we move to the towers," Rajesh offers.

My fevered mind turns to the stony balconies at the top.

In the car once more, Ted fiddles with his camera lenses. I feel such disgust for him, how feeble and gormless he strikes me just now when we are in such peril. Why can he not see it?

The driver parks the car along the edge of the gravel lane. They lead us to Kirti Stambh, the shorter, but no less ornate, of the two famed towers. The outside is studded with sculptures of curvy women holding musical instruments, and serene men with weapons.

Dilip allows us to enter first, and we climb the narrow steps up and up. Rajesh does not follow us in. Perhaps his role is to stay at the bottom to make sure when we're pushed over the balcony, we aren't able to get up and run off. The thought drives me up each of the fifty-four steps, my breath ragged, giving me a head start in assessing each floor we pass to better position myself for defense. On the top floor, I cower near the top of the stairs.

"Don't you want to see the view, dear?" Ted asks as he hastens past me to the balcony.

The guide gestures for me to approach, his body cocked and eyebrows raised. A gold chain dangles within the open *V* of his shirt, just above his exposed chest hair. With one eye steady on him, I inch toward the balcony, and quickly look down upon the surrounding countryside in one direction and the city we passed through on the other. I can see a temple not far in the distance, surrounded by lush trees with long, waxy yellow-green leaves.

There is nothing familiar here, so far from home. I think about our bird feeder in the back garden. We should have had someone fill it for us while we were gone; the poor birds. They'd be expecting us. This sudden urge to get back to fill the bird feeder is a physical ache between my shoulders. And what if we don't make it back? The birds will go hungry, the shrieks of their starving cries will go unheard.

Dilip never approaches us. He descends the steps first, warning us to hold the wall down the narrow descent. The image of his unexpected violence of a few hours ago explodes in my mind. His contorted face as he scolded and struck the bicyclist. Could this be *my* chance? Should I make a preemptive strike? Give him a good hard shove? By the time I work this through, I am concerned there are not enough steps or height left to finish the act properly. That, and the curving of the tower may stop his fall too soon, and at worst, he'd get a sprained ankle and mounted ire.

My body reacts before I come to a conclusion. I plant my foot and pretend to trip, falling forward slightly, and then I change my mind, but it is too late. I have shoved the guide after all, hard in the back with my shoulder. My balance is upset and I smack my bottom down on the hard stone. Dilip catapults forward with a startled gasp, saving himself a couple of steps later by hugging the wall.

Ted scrambles down the steps behind me and puts an arm around my waist to help me stand.

"I'm-I'm so sorry," I call down.

"No, ma'am. Is my fault." He walks up the few steps and takes my arm. "*I* am sorry for walking in your way. Here." He walks backward, leading me down several steps until I tug my hand free of his bony grip.

"I'm fine," I say, attempting to hide my trembling hands.

"Are you sure?" Ted asks. "Really, you must be more careful, pet. You could have killed the man."

"Bloody silly of me. Really, I'm fine," I say.

My legs are soft as lemon curd, but I make it down the stairs unassisted. Rajesh stands at the bottom, his mouth agape and brows furrowed. Dilip chuckles and attempts to smooth his hair back into place as he says something to Rajesh in Hindi.

Ted takes my arm on one side, and I find the sturdy arm of our guide on the other as they lead me to the car. Is Dilip limping? I hear Ted gently tell the driver we'd best pack it in for the day.

"Of course. We are understanding," he says with a bobble of his head. "Heat and travel is too much overwhelming in India."

The driver starts the car as I am tucked inside.

"What is it, pet?"

I lean away from him, against the door frame. I take off my hat and put it in my lap. I am depleted. As the car moves forward, the air plays on my face. I swallow a great sob, a drowned noise sneaking out.

Rajesh turns the radio on to raucous cheering. A commentator announces in a mixture of Hindi and English the overs, runs, and wickets in a cricket match, the baller coming in from the south end. The thwack of a cricket bat. I catch my breath at the unbidden image of Marcus and Ted in the back garden. Marcus bowling to his dad, his little legs running forward, his arm spiraling wildly to let loose the ball. The acrobatics Ted endured to hit those balls.

The memory hits me with sudden joy, akin to rounding a corner and coming upon a deer on the walking path. Beside me, Ted rests his hand on mine, and I grasp it.

Ted doesn't find remembering as painful as I do. Our son was murdered. I can't forget that for even a moment. How can he? How can he bear to project images of Marcus onto the living room wall? I suddenly recall, a few months ago, I overheard Ted in conversation with the greengrocer at the shop in midtown. I heard him telling a treasured story about Marcus, a story that didn't involve his death. Ted had been smiling, and he made the clerk laugh. I felt betrayed at the time, and now I understand why.

When I think about Marcus' death, I am attempting to share the pain and fear Marcus must have felt. The pain and fear I could not prevent. But how can I surmount the tragedy of Marcus' death and remember his life instead, like Ted?

I free another memory. The time Marcus got into my makeup. He had just turned three, and he had been so proud to show off his artwork on the clawfoot tub and the bathroom walls.

The time he and I went to Pleasure Beach on our own. How strong and cold the winds were, blowing off the North Sea. Even so, he rode a donkey along the beach, and splashed in the frigid water. Afterward, I bundled him in towels and held him in my arms until his teeth stopped chattering.

I come up with another memory. And another. I'm testing the water. Yes, it hurts, still ever so tender. But there is joy there amidst the pain. I cover my face with my hands, it's too much at once. Silent tears streak down my face.

Ted slides a hand around my shoulders and leans lightly into me. I look up at him. "He was so beautiful," I whisper. "It hurts."

"I know, love. I'm so sorry."

I realize how kind, how tolerant Ted has been. He's been my anchor, I just didn't know it. Instead, I resented him for it. It took leaving my familiar, where I knew what was around every corner, where I controlled my environment, to unearth what I had held inside.

As we pass the fifth gate on our descent from the hill complex, I begin to untangle. I am waking from a dream in which there was so much activity I never really slept. A nightmare in which I tried to kill a man.

The site is suddenly teeming with people laden with backpacks, cameras, tripods, guidebooks. Where did they come from? Have they been here the whole time? There are people on foot, in cars, and in belching rickshaws, gawking up at the temples, towers, and palaces, awestruck. I too want to own this rapture. I want to imagine myself a warrior out on the plains, forging gloriously towards certain death at the hands of invaders. I want to imagine I am the maharani assaying my kingdom from the highest tower. Instead, I have acted like a once imperious noblewoman, now skittering through corridors.

As soon as we reach the city center, we idle in traffic. The narrow road is clogged with wheeled vehicles, people on foot, as well as bicycles, and carts pulled by man and beast alike. It is a cacophony of noise, color, and smell. From the corner of my eye, I see a figure darting between it all. A girl, barefoot, in a faded dress. She heads right toward our car as if she is expecting us—or we are expecting her.

She approaches the car and curls her fingers around the door frame of the open window. The girl beams at our guide through her dirt-streaked face. She wears a dulled, gold orb in one nostril.

"Arre wah!" Dilip exclaims. "You grew like a tree since last we saw you!"

She looks behind him to where we sit in the backseat and gives us the same smile, a smile that belies the struggle her life must be. She has a front tooth missing, the beginnings of a tooth coming in.

"Hang about," Ted says.

He is pulling his wallet from his pants pocket, but Dilip has thrust a two-tier tiffin carrier, each tin the size of finger bowls, into the girl's arms. She blows a kiss to him, and with a free hand tosses a marigold into my lap. Traffic inches forward and she skips backward, away from our car. She kisses her hand again, and then again, throwing her joy in our direction. She vanishes into the throng.

"How about that, then," Ted says.

"Sharma is one of many beggar children," Rajesh says. "She knows Dilip-Bhai is too much generous with his lunch. Not me!" He pats his belly.

A murky, reflected version of our driver through the side mirror reveals the gap between his teeth which gives him a look of innocence I hadn't noticed before. I look to our guide, the side of his face in repose, a thoughtful, faraway smile pulling at the lips beneath his moustache. No evidence of suspicion, or accusation in his expression. He appears wistful, if anything. Maybe he is thinking of loved ones at home, maybe even a little girl about Sharma's age.

Just then, he turns to the back seat expectantly. Rajesh smiles at me through the rearview mirror as Dilip asks, "Did you enjoy this utmost beauty of our country, madam?"

I look out the window, and I am able to smile. I can see beyond, and through the morass of my memory.

"Yes," I answer, clutching the marigold. "I most certainly did."

SPIDERS
By Thomas Brown

"HERMIT SPIDER, READY FOR insertion."

I felt my eyelids involuntarily flutter. The last of the Real was the taste of the strawberry biteguard. It gave me the limited promise that whatever was inside waiting for me, no matter how bad it was, maybe the pain I felt in the construct wouldn't make me bite my own goddamned tongue off. Or die. It was on the menu, after all. Sex and death, baby, someone always died.

"I'm in," I whispered into my earpiece. Neon reflected off of everything, the windows, the screens, the permanently damp streets. The air hummed with electricity, with random thoughts from the uncontrolled Id that hovered at the barest edges of my attention. It noticed me the moment I stepped foot in the city, and I was betting it didn't like that I was there.

"What do you see?" questioned the voice in my ear. Green already had a nagging tone about him.

I looked at a passerby, dark suit, long hair, katana slung on his back. He eyed me and spit his toothpick on the ground in disgust as he passed me by. A nano later, I eyed my reflection and saw my suit was a replica. The length of my hair, the color red draining away to the matching black. A toothpick packed tight against my cheek. I had brought my own katana.

I moved through the crowd, brushing into a woman barely five feet tall, maybe eighty years old. She stepped lively in a pair of traditional wooden geta sandals that looked beyond uncomfortable. But I had to smile, because she also wore a katana. Everyone did. I did my best to look Yakuza, both stoic and lackadaisical. To be honest, I knew little more than the Drive's construct did.

I walked a block as Green did his best to get me killed by telling me fuck all about my op. Who gave a shit what I saw? He should already know the danger level of the Drive with everyone armed.

A dark alley ahead, an undeveloped knuckle in the construct. I took the second to hope that no one would see me inside, and I turned down it to respond to Captain Fucknut.

"Shut up. What level of Kenjutsu is this Drive?"

"Um, I don't know, I'm just following—"

"Do as I tell you. Go to the Drive index and look up the level. I'm dark for an unknown amount of time, I need to know this now, numb nuts."

"Ma'am, this is a basic retrieval before—"

"Listen, shitbird. While you are checking the Kenjutsu level, when was the last access point on this Drive?

I heard the whistle of steel being unsheathed before I saw her. It was the old woman. She had made me, the little old bitch. I rolled to the sound and drew my blade from my back and made a horizontal strike across the old woman's torso, sending her two halves spinning in different directions.

She was dead before she hit the ground, but that was of little reassurance. If she made me, then…

"Enemy of the Tetsuo Shogunate, lower your blade and meet our good justice with honor."

I stepped out of the knuckle and spoke to Green through my earpiece.

"Well, it doesn't matter now. I am in what looks like the mid-21st, a representation of a Tokyo Prefecture. In front of me are about forty men and women with katanas drawn looking to cut me up. The level of Kenjutsu sword training is moot as fuck all. We will have words, you and I, if I survive this."

"Y-y-yes, ma'am. This Drive is solely for archive use, ten extended generations. No access points beyond archive points after creation."

One hundred years since anyone had accessed this Drive for anything other than to archive? A century? How could anyone even be alive to care about what was on it? Floors below me lay thousands of Drives—people in stasis, their brains turned into short term, unhackable storage that was DNA coded. Besides the owner, the only person who could get in was by direct connection, a Spider, like me. But the owner just kept archiving, copying to a new Drive every decade, gen after gen, never looking back.

For a nano it gave me pause, but really, what did it matter? I wasn't likely to live through the night anyhow.

I eyed the many blades. Someone held up a warrant for me to surrender. A light rain fell as I stepped out into the street, hugging the wall so no one could get cute and ninja me in the ass, but I didn't have long.

"You are an enemy of the state, drop your sword, meet your fate with honor," said the man with the warrant. He seemed like a minor bureaucrat from any one of a hundred samurai movies, the ones who always start the troubles that escalate into god knows what.

Then it clicked. He *was* that bureaucracy. They were the Yakuza. Somewhere there were ninjas. It was a game, and I had entered the first level.

I slashed through the warrant with a single cut and took his hand with it. Then, I tested the construct. I ran forward as the first wave of swords raised, and looked for the biggest, baddest one in the bunch. Sumo-ring huge with a club rather than a sword, his hair drawn back in a tight bun, I ran at him—junior boss by my guess. Once he engaged, the others would pause. He was yelling at me and swinging his club over his head and it thundered into the spot I had just been. I heard pavement shatter under the blow.

I hadn't waited for him. The construct existed inside a Drive. You aren't even breathing. If you aren't breathing, then the laws of physics aren't part of the construct. There are limits, of course. Superman doesn't exist, and you can't really fly, because the mind will always fuck you over and remind you about gravity. Eventually.

But I could make a lightning fast, ninety-degree turn on a

heel and then another and another. In the Real, I would fall. I probably couldn't make the first turn without tearing up my knee or something worse. In Construct Tokyo, I made three in the time it takes a heart to flutter most of a beat. Three nineties, and I stepped behind the Sumo and drew my katana between his legs, up through his body and back into the wet evening air.

A single drop of blood blended into the rainwater that ran off the polished waves of the blue steel blade.

He needed to look back at me as if nothing had happened. It was a trope, after all.

"Ha, you missed, you—" The red line ran down the center of his face. I saw the wide eyes of shock and didn't wait. I could already hear the ridiculous spray of blood fill the air behind me as I cut into the rest of the shocked anonymous ranks like I was hacking my way through a rainforest jungle.

"Hermit to Green. This archive is not meant to be accessed by anyone but the owner, you sad sack of shit. The construct is acting like an infection system and is actively hunting me. This is a cluster fuck and a half. Get me out of here."

"Um, um, that, that is a negative Hermit. The mission is critical. I am running a trace and—"

"I am under attack by a wave system, I beat the first boss, and I am going out of order. That means the construct will deviate from its own protocols, you spineless little cock turd. I am killing Yakuza right now. God knows what is next. Now get me out of here!"

I rolled under a horizontal blow and sliced through a woman's ankles, then spun to a knee and disemboweled what looked like a half cowboy, half Japanese gangster. All black with cowboy hat and boots. He had some style, and I nodded in approval as his body flipped backward like a Pez dispenser.

"Hermit. I am not authorized to pull you out. I couldn't even if I wanted to. Instructions in this situation are to, um, find high ground, and—"

"And I swear to god I will cut your dick off to prevent future contamination of the fucking gene pool, Green. Oh, fuck!"

I burst through the Yakuza pack. A tall samurai in traditional clothing and an old man leaning on a cane stood nearby, eyes wild with crazy. Suddenly the sun was in my face and the rain slowed.

Of course.

The old man grunted at me in Japanese, but the voice I heard didn't match his lips.

Someone had dubbed over his voice.

I didn't listen; there was no need. I had seen the goddamned movie. The sun was in my eyes, to his back, and he was telling me his son was about to kill me, blah, blah, blah. But the construct was still mine to play with. I tried to summon a gun and Indy my way out, but no such luck.

Fine, I was gonna have to work for it.

I took a quick glance over my shoulder. All the random crazies back there had given this new boss some space to behead me. Ninja ran vertically up the gleaming glass and neon. Combatants from other, even more obscure Asian genres appeared at the edge of the crowd. The longer I waited to engage the samurai, the more diverse and impatient the construct would become.

I held my blade out in my hand, the edge an inch from the pavement, and charged the samurai. He ran at me. I saw only his silhouette; the rest of my target was crowded out by the glare of the duelist's sun, but that was, of course, intentional. I was the hero. The goddamned construct just didn't know it. The hero had an ace up her sleeve. In the movie it had been a little boy on the hero's shoulders with a reflector attached to his tiny top knot.

Racing across the wet pavement, I imagined a hair scrunchie wrapping around my soaking wet red hair with the same reflector on it. I wanted my original hair color back for this. The samurai's hand involuntarily lifted to block the sun. My blade cut through meat and bone so fast it could only be a movie. Or a game. Or a one hundred-year-old construct within a Drive.

The head tumbled from his shoulders, and blood spit three feet into the air as the old man mumbled at me in two different languages.

I ran like hell.

A whistle in the wind told me something was cutting through it. A back flip landed me on a parked, century-old black sedan as shurikens and arrows hurtled past me. I parried like a baseball player slapping away foul after foul, looking for a way out, somewhere to go.

I needed to access the archive and complete my mission if dickless wasn't going to let me out. Up and down the hoods and trunks of cars, I ran faster than the mixed assemblage behind me. Down the street was an intersection.

"Alright, you little cock-knocking rent boy, I need an access point to the archive. Everything looks the same here. Except for all the people trying to kill me." Nothing. "Goddamnit Green, where is the fucking access point?"

"There is no access point." The voice had changed, cool and controlled. A voice I knew nearly as well as that of my own mother's. Sometimes she acted as though she was. "The owner of the Drive never intended to have the Drive opened by anyone but himself. His access points are in the form of quest helpers. NPCs. Non-Player Characters. We are reorienting your location. Head east and search for the avatar. We have no idea what it will look like, but it will make itself known."

I reached the intersection and sprinted east. "Copy, Bird. What is going on? Why am I locked in here?"

"I don't know. I'm working on it. I received the alert when you went in and came in right away. The owner is on his way to us. You were his request. Just survive. I will monitor you the rest of the way. And you will, I repeat, will apologize to Green when you get out for threatening to kill him when you get out."

I recalibrated my readings and shook my head to her comment, knowing she couldn't see.

"Yes, you will."

I smiled, and it made me lose my focus. I got cocky. Cocky kills in the construct as much as it does in the Real.

A black sedan less than five meters away lit up, and glass blew everywhere. The car behind it caught fire. The explosion knocked me off my feet and threw me back into the side of an identical black sedan. As I peeled myself from the aluminum imprint of my body, pain sliced through my shoulder. A jagged piece of metal lodged deep. I let out a feral growl as I yanked it out and willed it to heal. Then I heard a voice with a thick Austrian accent.

"If she bleeds, we can kill her!"

The construct had drawn the next round of playthings for me. Four of them were in mock soldier outfits, pointing a massive array of guns in my direction. I didn't wait for the next one-liner as all four of them opened fire.

They moved fast, but I moved faster. I imagined the wads of lead were droplets of rain, and I danced between them, around them, and finally over them as I jumped and spun in the air, landing behind the big man who had been swinging a rolling barrel Mini Gun from side to side. I rammed my sword through the back of his head until the hilt rested at the base of his skull and turned him around like a puppet on a wire.

"I don't got time to bleed!"

The muscular man's gun blasted his surprised friends to pieces at close range. I pried the gun out of his dead hands and took aim at the remaining Yakuza and ninja who couldn't catch a fucking hint. I gave over to a Valkyrie rage as cars exploded and bodies fell all around me. Explosions lined the street. Shattered glass filled the air. Bullets and fire would fill the space until the job was done. Bullets never ran out until the task was complete.

I noticed a pair of men dressed like undercover cops dive for cover behind a shattered car.

No favorites, no good guys.

I riddled the car they hid behind and then laid down a thick hail of bullets across the rest of the street until nothing else moved. The rotating barrels clicked empty, leaving the electronic whir of the six spinning barrels. I dropped the massive gun that in the Real I never would have been able to pick up, much less manipulate with any skill.

Have katana, will travel.

I hit the next intersection at a sprint.

"Bird, I need a quest helper. How about something that doesn't want to kill me!"

"Searching," came back her voice. "Hit the alley on the right."

"Copy."

I almost overran the entrance to the alley, sliding into it. A man with reckless hair and a crazed smile, dressed in a black suit, stood in the alleyway. He had a hammer in his hand, and the light glinted off the handle of a blade sticking from his shoulder. At his feet were the bodies of several men. I hugged the wall and waited for an attack, but he laughed and ran past. Another reference, this one I didn't know. I shook it off and looked amongst the bodies, wondering if crazy pants had killed my lead.

The alley was empty of all life but a goddamned cat.

"Bird, I have a few bodies." I was certain I had missed the NPC. "There isn't a soul in the fucking alley but a mangy fucking cat."

With that, the cat looked up at me. It glowed a golden light.

"Never mind, Bird."

I picked the cat up.

"I need the file repository, where is it?"

The cat, a tabby with an attitude, growled and took a swipe at me. Or so I thought. My wrist map lit up with an arrow and the quest appeared on my HUD. I heard the click-clack of a racked shotgun and spun to see the undercover cops. I used the only weapon in hand and threw the tabby at the cops, then trucked down the alley.

Hissing and swearing in Chinese sounded behind me. I followed the arrow on my HUD as I read the quest riddle.

Dear Boss,

I keep hearing I've been caught and what you want has been found, but I'm still here. Find me if you can, before I find you. I like my games, and if you are reading this, then you want to play, too. Squeal if you must, my knife is a sharp one. See you soon.

Good Luck. Yours Truly,

Jack

From Hell

What the fuck? I finished reading the quest and I passed through a cloud and my boots click-clacked on a different pavement entirely. But it wasn't a cloud, it was fog. And I wasn't in Tokyo anymore.

"Shit on me. I got a quest from some guy named Jack from Hell. I think I'm in the past. Maybe in Europe. He says he has a knife. Who the hell am I looking for?"

Bird laughed, and it made me uneasy.

"Is there fog, cobblestone streets, everything looks wet, and it smells?"

A woman wearing a dress I couldn't, *wouldn't*, match walked past me. I wasn't blending in on this one.

"Yes, there is the familiar aroma of shit. Am I in London?"

"I do not know how you missed Jack the Ripper in your education, but yes. Late nineteenth century serial killer in London. Very dangerous. He likes prostitutes."

"Oh, Jesus H, can't I just kill all the men in the construct?"

She exhaled slowly. That was a no. So I followed the arrow, hoping it was leading me to this Jack asshole. I had programed my studies to include heroes, warriors, soldiers. I'd left out true crime.

I had been a Drive, once upon a time. Unlike most people, I made my own way in the world and used my decade to learn every damned programming language and more math than was conceivable. Add in a lifetime of fighting skills, and I became a Spider instead of a fucking tool.

The air was thick and tasted like what I assumed soot tasted like.

Even the unreal, so absolutely unreal in every way, can feel like reality to the mind. The moisture in the air, the ambient noises of people talking, a horse-drawn cart rolling down the street, shit hitting the street as it passed. I wondered if the construct did that intentionally as a distraction or if it was procedurally generated to give the world life.

This construct was one of the most sophisticated I had seen. Certainly, for something so old. It was generations ahead of its time.

I heard footsteps behind me. I spun with my blade in hand, ready to take heads.

Her eyes were wide with fright.

I lowered my blade.

"Sorry. My bad. You wouldn't know some bastard named Jack, would you?"

It was a joke, but her mouth bounced up and down with no words coming out. She wasn't quaking in fear of me.

Fuck.

I ducked and rolled into the street as the blade whisked through the air above me. A man laughed, and I heard a gurgling sound come from the woman's throat as his blade sliced her instead of me. She was a simulation, always intended to be in the wrong place at the wrong time, but a part of me still felt bad for it.

Jack laughed away, a maniacal caricature of a villain, hacking and slashing at me as he chased me into the street.

"Come along poppet, you were looking for me. Am I not everything you were looking for, desiring?"

He moved blindingly fast. Another boss, the fastest so far. He was strong, too, and as I deflected his blows, I looked to break away and give myself enough space to use the sword as the good lord of samurai intended me to use it.

He giggled as his knife, long and gleaming in the gaslight, clanged off of my sword again and again. I allowed him to dictate the terms of the fight, "fell" backward and gave him a good solid to the nethers. He doubled over almost instantly. Good to know nothing was spared on the details of the coding.

With a half whimper, half growl, he tried to straighten up, the knife loose in a black gloved hand.

"Girl, I'll…"

Click-clack! Boom!

The shotgun blast hit Jack square in the back, but the action sequence announcement—the blast—had already prepared me for the two undercover cops still hunting me from Neo Tokyo.

Jack lurched forward, and I rolled to my side and kicked the falling knife at the first cop I saw. Black suit. White shirt. Sharp and sexy, and the shock on his face as the blade spun in the air and buried itself in his shoulder was the break I needed.

His rough cop buddy fired wildly. I rolled into a cartwheel and spun into a nearby alley while he yelled at me in frustration. I knew by his code he would catch his falling partner. They would say something witty to each other before the wounded one would send the other one ahead to fight the good fight. Or maybe he would just pull the knife out and make the construct play on for him. Anything was possible.

I looked at my wrist and saw that the arrow had stopped. There was nothing there.

"Bird, the Ripper asshole is dead, the route put me in an alley, and nothing is here, nothing is here goddamnit!"

I spun in a circle and saw nothing but fog and brick walls tricked out in graffiti. The graffiti…

I reached for my lenses. Night vision, infra-red, and then childish black light, and I saw a symbol I recognized. I should, it was the most well-known corp symbol in the world, a bisected Mobius strip with a W in the middle. The Infinite Wilson. I should damned well know the mark, I was using his tech.

I stepped back and read the words.

"Wilson is the man that will not be blamed for nothing."

My HUD pinged as I read the words. A new arrow pointed me down the alley. Just in time. A gun safety clicked off behind me and bullets ripped into the walls and ground. The cop I had injured was wounded but still up for a fight, even with a broken wing. I ran down the alley and turned toward another wet London street. Before I hit the bricks, the second cop ran past on the street. He was racing to get ahead of me, and seeing me, grabbed the edge of the brick wall to pull himself back.

Face meet sword pommel! I couldn't kill Chow Yun Fat, even if he wasn't real. Nearly one-hundred-years-dead, and he was still too badass to kill. I couldn't have lived with myself. But hitting him hard upside the head was just fine. I heard him hit the road behind me and gasp and never looked back.

Shops and stores lined the road. Close. So close. The arrow on my HUD and wrist dove tailed together to my left. The access point was meters away. That was usually when the ground fell out from under my feet, but I kept going, relentless. The next attack could come any second. My boots were loud on the wet cobblestones. Meter by meter, the arrow shortened until I climbed a set of worn sandstone stairs. I looked at the doors and grabbed the handle.

"The Rotting Moor Antiquarian Books."

A twist of my wrist and I was inside and I slammed the door behind me.

Not a second later the two hard-boiled cops, guns in hands,

were there, glaring at me through the glass door.

In the movie, Chow's character name was Tequila. He always had a toothpick in his mouth, and he spit it out in anger at the door. I readied myself for the next fight.

But it didn't happen.

Instead, both of them smiled and gave me a thumbs up. They waved and turned around, clapping each other on their shoulders like a job well done, and walked away. I had reached an archive, and the construct wouldn't endanger the information inside. Of course, idiot.

"This is Hermit. I'm in. Beginning search protocol."

"Copy Hermit. We will extract directly from there. Drive owner has arrived. Download the files. He has requested your presence."

"Uh, roger Bird."

What the fuck?

So the room was the extraction point.

I rested my hands on the countertop, and an old loop of a magnifying glass manifested. I held it up, feeling the elation of the beginning of the end, as one of only a handful of people in the system who could be standing where I was. But I so intensely wanted to be angry as well.

He had trapped me inside. Did the Drive owner know what he was asking for when he said he wanted to meet me? Bastard.

I looked on a shelf behind the counter with the magnifying glass, feeling drawn to it. I bunny hopped over the counter and pawed through a pile of papers and pulled out a pack of—what?

Five hard plastic objects were rubber banded together, and

they looked ancient. I didn't recognize the tech, except to know it was really old. Each object had a metal piece that snapped back and forth at the bottom. I knew they were just a representation of something, a file, but I was still curious. That and the name, written by hand, faded in black marker.

"What is DOOM?"

There was silence on the other end. I didn't like the quiet. Then, "The file you have is the target. Size is, wait, how can anything be that small? Perhaps it is just a picture? Irrelevant. Mission is a success. I'm pulling you out. Prepare for transfer to the Real. He's here, anyhow."

I felt my eyelids flutter involuntarily as they reconstructed my impression of reality. I always wondered if I was ever really in the Real. A well-built construct in a modern Drive was almost impossible to discern from the Real. Only my implants told me there was a difference. What if they didn't know or were told a lie? Would it matter?

Psycho fucking babble. I would be three beers into it in an hour, and I wouldn't care.

My eyelids locked open. The soft, heavily padded table I lay on rotated up and I spit my biteguard onto the ground. I grabbed the guide rail on the table as my reality stabilized, and I looked down at my hand. The plastic squares with "DOOM" written on them were still there in holo form. I glanced up to the observation windows and saw the unsmiling face of Bird, tall with her military cut blonde hair, impatiently waiting for me.

"Yeah, yeah, boss."

I tossed the pack through the air, and the holo hit the glass and disappeared.

"Files online and compiled. Finding compatibility mode for files," said some tech in my ear.

"Good job, Hermit. Come up. Your presence is requested," said Bird.

I stretched and rubbed all the places the construct had hurt me—though I hadn't really been hurt—and walked to the steps. I wanted to hit the showers and get out of my crawl suit. The brain and the body burned calories like an athlete when you are down, and I smelled like the better part of the Houston Rollerball team. But I knew an order when I heard it.

I opened the door to see what looked like half an ER med team and half a tactical security squad surrounding a man so old he was barely alive. Wires and tubes penetrated his withered bare chest as he sat in a bed focused on a wide monitor. Bird waved me forward. He used a holo keyboard to do something as he swore at the screen.

On the far side of the room, doing his best to ignore my arrival, stood Green. I gave him a quick glare that said our business wasn't done, and he buried his face in a console, probably hoping I would dry up and blow away. Dream on, fuck wit.

"Sonofabitch! Should have killed you. Bullshit!"

The old guy was ancient, but there was grit to his voice. He wheezed after the moment. A doctor stepped toward him, and he waved him off.

"No! This is why I'm here. This and her. Come here young

lady, sit down next to me, cough, cough!" His body shook with the cough, but he fought it. I sat down next to him and saw what he was doing.

It was a game. Heavily pixelated, so old, but I could immediately tell he was the protagonist, and there were demons, and he was shooting them with all manner of guns.

"This is 'DOOM' young lady. This is what you risked your life to retrieve for me."

I was immediately fucking pissed.

"You sonuvabitch!"

"Yes, I am. But you had to see. And I wanted to finish what I started. Won't be apologizing. I never have. Lost my wife over my inability to say it, I will not start now. I'm Jack Wilson if you hadn't guessed. Technically, you have worked for me your entire life. Everyone in this room works for me. Most of this tech is mine. So humor me for a few last minutes."

I looked at the old man more closely. A few wisps of red hair still clung to his otherwise bald head. He wasn't on the cocktail. He was too old for it; it wouldn't have worked on him. The tubes connecting him to the bed seemed to be doing battle themselves, keeping the old man alive.

His attention never wavered from the game, but he spoke to me.

"Most of the internal organs failed in my nineties, but I had no interest in dying. So I replaced them one by one. 'More machine than man...'"

"Are you twisted and evil?" I asked, finishing the line from *Star Wars*.

"I was told you love movies, just like me. No, I'm not. But I could have been a better man. A better person. So much better. When I was comparatively young, my wife and daughter left me. I wasn't that nice to be around. All I did was work. I saw to their comfort, their safety, their future. The last time I spoke to my daughter was more than a century ago. Much more than a century ago."

His hands had a tremor when he coughed, which was often, and he seemed to sneer at his own weakness as he continued to play the game. His focus stayed on the game as the pixels turned to red exploding giblets, his guns finding target after target.

"I was a loner in college, sort of. We were all loners, banded together by a mutual love of things that eventually took over the world. Japanese animation, video games, comics, some things lost to time, like this game. I came from a small town in the middle of farm country, but I never went back after I left for school. I discovered my world there. At a place that doesn't even exist anymore.

"On the morning of my graduation, I went to a place called Baker Systems. A twenty-four-hour computer lab where you could install your own software on a computer. Eight in the morning I went there and installed 'DOOM' on a computer and started a game. This game. On June 5th 1996. I felt the hands of a girl, a woman, on my shoulders, a kiss on my cheek. Around nine, whispering in my ear, she told me if I ever wanted to graduate, I needed to follow her. That I could finish the silly game any time.

"I would have followed her anywhere, but, but she didn't make it. But I'm going to finish the game. One last thing to do. Before

I join her."

His breathing came faster, and I heard his pulse race on the machine and I saw people scramble around him.

"Fuck off all of you. Hermit, tell them to let me finish."

I'd formed an instant partnership with one of the most powerful men on the planet. I didn't hesitate.

"He knows what he's doing, and you heard him, back off, way off." I mimicked his tone with a layer of my own and watched as what looked like a brain with four legs attacked Wilson's avatar.

"This is the BFG. It stands for—"

"Big fucking gun," I said with a smile.

"Yeah kid, yeah."

Even with the shake and the frailty, he danced back and forth until the brain split in pixelated two and the creature died. His avatar ran around for another minute until he hit the center of the screen. There didn't seem to be anything left to kill, and the screen fell away and a coda appeared, telling the end of the story. The old man didn't care. Mission accomplished.

"Roads not traveled. I went and graduated. Sat next to Heather. Certain she and I would be together forever, but, yeah. She didn't make it. I met another woman, someone I should have loved better, had a daughter, well it doesn't matter." Leaning back on the bed, he smiled at me. He was fading fast and waved everyone off. He had done what he had come for.

"The pad."

An assistant handed him an oPad that darkened with his touch, and he took a pen and signed something.

"When you became a Drive for a decade, you could have become a doctor, an engineer, a fucking rocket scientist, instead you became a Spider. Why?"

"It's my mind, my body. If I'm going to give up a decade of my life, I'll get out of it what I want, not what I'm told to want."

He smiled again as his life faded.

"Good for you. I'm sorry, Hermit, sorry for not meeting you earlier, sorry for just being me. But there's always tomorrow." He looked at the screen as the credits rolled, a single tear streaking down his face, and he shook his head once. He leaned to me and whispered on his last breath, "Fuck Rosebud," and fell back on the bed dead.

No one made a move towards him.

"Isn't someone going to do something. Anything?"

"No," said a man in a suit. "This was the wish of your Great-Great Grand Father. You now possess all that was once his. But I must ask before we go further, what is Rosebud?"

I looked at the suit and shook my head, not understanding completely what had just happened, but understanding enough.

"It's not for you. It's not for any of us," was all I had for him.

HAN SOLO, MASKED
By Cody Bok

HE TURNED ON THE porch light, and there it was.

Jason stepped out into the late dusk of the city. The package lay there, long and brown, across the front porch of his rented bungalow. It held within it a heavy-duty cardboard cutout of Han Solo, which Jason had bought right after the stay-at-home orders were issued. Apparently, so did everyone else. It didn't matter. After two months of waiting, Han had arrived. His cardboard frame stood at an imposing 6'1", at least according to the seller's description. Jason stood against the cutout and pressed his hand on top of his head to estimate the height difference. Jason was about three inches shorter. Seemed right.

Jason assembled the prop kit so Han could stand on his own. While thinking of how to best show him off, Jason sent his dad a picture of the cardboard scoundrel standing in the corner of the living room. He peeked out his window to the neighbors' yard. Balloons and signs advertised a kid's birthday, unmissable with their radiant sheen and tropical colors. An idea formed.

The next afternoon, Jason set Han, with a newly affixed mask over his nose and mouth, on the porch. He also placed a sign out front with a bold arrow pointing toward Han that read: "Han Shoots First if YOU Aren't Wearing a Mask!" The Kessel Run record holder was outside in time for Thursday evening's not-quite-the-usual-level-of-rush hour.

Fortified by a pile of rocks at his base, Han overlooked the road from underneath the porch's overhang. Jason passed him on his way out to the old Camry, carrying an overnight bag (really just an old backpack) for a weekend trip south of Indy to visit his parents.

Jason watched the crisp fall leaves undulate across the hills as he drove. He had planned to hike the hills with Dad, but it rained all weekend. Instead, they watched the original Star Wars trilogy—Dad in his chair, Jason on the couch. Tradition. Dad got out the lightsaber he had bought for Jason one childhood Christmas. It was now a faded and splotchy lime green, but it still made the nostalgic SWOOSH as it sliced through the air. Before Jason left, Dad asked if he wanted to take the lightsaber home. (He asked every visit.) Jason looked at it, smiled ruefully, and shook his head.

"Nah, you keep it."

When Jason got home, Han lay in the front yard. Jason bent over him. The bubbling rumples characteristic of wet cardboard rolled across Han like waves. He rubbed his thumb over Han's hair. The printed surface pilled and curled into a thin cardboard burrito, leaving a brown bald spot on his head. He also fingered the pen-sized puncture through Han's forehead. Someone had written on his sign, too: "I shot first, because I ain't wearing no fucking mask."

Jason picked up Han, carried him to the porch, and laid him down. He went inside and turned off the porch light.

RAINBOW'S BRIDGE
By Anne Johnston

BEYOND THE CRACKED SIDEWALK, and the telephone pole with layers of flyers in a rainbow of colors, and the patch of dry brown grass, there stood a ten-foot high concrete block wall, caked with layers of old paint. There was a small shrine at the foot of it, with burnt-out candles and dead flowers and a few soggy pet toys. One word of graffiti filled the wall, red letters on a gold background: Rejoice!

Rainbow tilted her head to match the angle of the word. It was a new addition, and she wasn't certain what it implied about the expectations of those who came here to call upon her. She shrugged one shoulder and crossed the empty street and lot. The glass jars of the candles and gold-toned bangles on some of the offerings caught the light as she approached the shrine. It glinted off of the broken glass in the surrounding lot and rebounded from the multi-hued, mostly golden wall. She paused to adjust the lay of a pair of tags on one of the collars and rolled a little jingle bell on a string free of the bouquet it had been wrapped around.

Then, without hesitation, Rainbow gave a slight flick of the tip of her long pony-tail, and an illuminated prism of solid air appeared. She strode confidently up the height of the wall and stepped lightly to its edge.

This monument to her had been around longer than any she remembered from the bygone era of her life in Greece and Rome. They had crumbled years ago. As a spirit of travel, she'd been used to simple offerings at the side of well-travelled paths and near inns. Their transitory nature had resonated better with her, but such shrines had not existed since the time of Solomon.

She looked down at the little pile of discarded treasures and rolled her eyes. Being bound to this plane by King Solomon and forced into servitude as a djinn was bad enough. To now be attached to such a paltry place, even one gilded with well-intentioned platitudes and gifts, made her spirit sink. The feeling was fleeting, however, as her hand grazed the locket attached to her wrist and reminded her that being bound to this plane did not mean she was bound to any particular person or place.

Her smile flooded the area with new radiance. Rainbow pirouetted along the thin edge of the wall. Pausing, she looked out at the horizon. She considered taking off toward it at top speed. She enjoyed racing the light, and her eyes brightened at the thought of another round, but she had never won. Realistically—an adjective that typically ran counter to Rainbow's very nature—she knew this time would be no different. Plus, her skin felt tight. She was in need of a real release. It had been, what, at least a month since she'd last granted a wish. The tension of unmet, wish-granting potential and unlimited power buzzed beneath her skin, and she shook her head against the idea of flitting off again. If she didn't find a way to let off some of the power build-up inside of her soon, it would literally make her crazy. And she needed to stay in her right mind if she was to stay free. Not many still believed in djinn, but those who did hunted for them and their lamps relentlessly. She couldn't afford to slip up.

Bouncing on the balls of her feet, she tore her eyes away from the allure of the horizon, and instead focused on the offerings below her. Rainbow quickly dismissed them. She felt the residual energy of the wishes the worshippers had imbued the items with but nothing specific enough to grant. Time and rain had washed away their spells.

Rainbow was undeterred. Amid the bleak landscape, her golden wall glowed. The mildly electric scent of recent storms energized the area, and lingering droplets in the sky caught the sunlight to cast her namesake far overhead for all to see. She needed only to be patient.

After chasing butterflies along the wall for a few hours and listening to the wishes of the depressingly small number of visitors, Rainbow mulled over her options. Most of the people who appeared asked for their pet to be safely and painlessly escorted "over the rainbow bridge." It was a sad request and not one which required any real expenditure of power. Even granting them all would only slightly ease the pressure under her skin. She had hoped for something more challenging, but djinn never could fulfill their own wishes. She sighed in resignation. One old man had tearfully begged his old beagle *not* be taken across. Rainbow focused on this request. Holding off death, granting miraculous recovery and longevity; these were tasks that, if done right, might be enough to let her go back to unfettered roaming for a while.

She was just solidifying in her mind the exact way in which to grant the wish, when a quiet voice floated up from the base of the wall. The woman who knelt there looked up, directly at Rainbow. Her wide, pleading eyes seemed to tap into Rainbow's own desires. As the hushed words of her prayer continued, a slithering chill slipped down Rainbow's spine. She shivered it away, certain the woman could not see her. Yet, she self-consciously checked that she hadn't disturbed something physical to accidentally have drawn attention. Seeing no obvious reason the woman might have seen through her veil, Rainbow again grasped the charm on her wrist—her transformed lamp—and cautiously stepped back down the wall to linger over the woman.

Rainbow peeked carefully around the now hunched form of the woman, who was crying and cradling something tenderly in her hands. The image of a lanky young man glared up at her from a school portrait. The edges of the photo paper had curled slightly from repeated handling, and a few creases marred the surface. Somehow the damage did nothing to diminish the striking features of the boy. His dark olive skin contrasted sharply with the crisp white shirt, and the tacky laser show background surprisingly managed to enhance the piercing blue of his eyes and the sheen of his tousled chestnut hair.

Rainbow cocked her head to look at the woman again and

saw the resemblance in her pronounced cheekbones and thin lips. Where his eyes were the blue of ocean depths, hers were the steel gray of warships. Even raining tears, they were the eyes of one who could weather anything. Rainbow's contemplation of the woman's character was suddenly shattered as those war-hardened eyes clenched shut. The woman clutched the picture to her chest and cried, "Please, protect him!"

With a dramatic sob, the woman set the picture down, leaning it against the glass-enclosed candle she'd brought. Rainbow watched her dust herself off, pull her shawl around her shoulders, and shuffle off across the lot. Once she was out of sight, Rainbow knelt and plucked the picture up. Although she hadn't been paying much attention to the woman's words, Rainbow could sense a deep longing attached to the image.

The boy had left and now had a job that kept him on the road, often in areas where he might be in danger. His mother had come to ask that he be protected on his journeys. Moreover, Rainbow sensed she was concerned he may not be on the right path in life. While Rainbow felt certain this was a rather typical maternal worry without need of her intervention to see things right in the end, it hinted at mystery and adventure. More so, at least, than continuing to be the grim reaper of pets.

Here was a wish that spoke to what she once was.

Using the desires laden on the picture, Rainbow fastened her intent on the young man and turned in the direction her magic told her he would be found. Walking into the sunset, memories of walking along the Appian Way with farmers traveling to market merged with those of crossing the Alps by elephant and roaming the American interstates with Kerouac. The nostalgia settled into a sepia-toned warmth around her.

She caught up to the boy in his dust-covered, little red truck at a convenience store as he pumped gas. It was not so far from the golden wall as she had expected, given his mother's concern about him having 'moved away.' But perhaps he was just starting his journey. It had become difficult for Rainbow to determine human age. He had filled out through the shoulders compared to his school picture but retained a fairly youthful face. He looked the right age to be heading to college or perhaps starting his first career. Rainbow shrugged. That must be it.

She climbed up into the bed of the truck as he hung up the pump. It jostled somewhat on its old shocks, and a loose can rattled. The boy looked back at the truck as it settled and quirked one dark eyebrow in Rainbow's direction. She froze. He pushed the gas tank flap closed and patted the edge of the truck absentmindedly. As he turned back to the cab, Rainbow let out a breath and sat down with her back against the tailgate.

Still shaken by how close she'd come to carelessly blowing her veil, Rainbow tugged on the charm around her wrist a few times as they pulled out of the gas station. Dizzy from the adrenaline rush, she didn't notice the truck pull into an alley behind a nearby restaurant. She was startled when the young man slammed his door. She could feel his desires roiling off of him in frustration as he stalked around the front of the truck and pulled open the passenger door.

As he dug around in the cab, Rainbow identified each of the boy's desires with slow consideration. He wanted to be recognized, which Rainbow assumed was true of most people, but it was more specific than a wish for general appreciation. There was a group the kid very much wanted to prove he belonged to. He saw this group as the first step to reaching his ultimate goals, which included becoming a prominent politician. He wanted the power to convince others and spread important messages across the world.

Rainbow felt caught up in the elation of these dreams, feelings so palpable she almost drew on her power to grant them without thinking. Then the boy reemerged from the cab and slapped a magnetic car-top sign onto the truck. He flicked a switch on its side and it glowed to life, garishly advertising "Pete's Pizza" in cracked red letters on a greenish background. Pizza delivery? This was the on-the-road job of danger the kid's mother wished her to protect him from? And this message he wanted to be delivery boy for, was it simply the gospel of stuffed-crust? The boy went in the backdoor of the restaurant and returned quickly with two black thermal bags full of pizza boxes.

As she had suspected, this was nothing but typical maternal worry, which did not require much expenditure of magic to put to rest. She might as well put a charm on the truck to protect the kid from vehicle accidents. She had solved the day's great mystery, would let off a little power by charming the truck, and might still have time to help out the old man's dog. At this rate, she'd be ready to race the light again by the time it showed up at dawn.

At the first stop light, she shifted to place her back against the cab of the truck. The rusty metal felt chalky as she let the magic seep through her fingers into it. The itching under her skin and dizziness in her head eased just a tad as she did so. The smell of warm rubber and asphalt assaulted her on the wind that rushed by, but the noise of rushing air had dulled noticeably compared to sitting against the tailgate.

From her new seat she could hear a recording of the "50 Greatest Speeches of US History." The narrator provided commentary on both the historical significance and the qualities of the speech that made it an enduring classic. Though interrupted by frequent stops for deliveries, the young man would restart and practice compelling parts of each speech several times. Rainbow sensed his need to flawlessly emulate these masters of persuasion.

So, she laced her magic delicately into his voice until it took on the timber of JFK's. She smiled as the boy exhorted, "What you can do for your coun—oh crap!" and was abruptly tossed around the bed as the truck tires squealed.

Rainbow peeked through the window on the back of the cab. A small dog lay injured on the pavement. The boy quickly ran back to the truck, grabbed his jacket from the cab, and lifted the body, delicately moving her onto the seat. Rainbow felt the familiar tug as the boy's unspoken wish about warding off death wove itself around her. She focused on the small dog's pained breathing as the truck rattled into the night, unconscious of how much time was passing. The dog was now Rainbow's focus, her little heartbeat a metronome, their lives melding to sustain the fragile canine body.

When the ride ended, she was lifted again. The kid slid her body onto a soft pile of clothing among the boxes in the garage. He pulled an old coat over the top, creating a cave that emanated the sweetness of old ladies who frequently powdered themselves—a light rose motif that played ironically well in the deep recesses of Rainbow's ancestral brain. The pizza kid lifted the dog's head to help her lap water from a hubcap. He broke bits of pepperoni and crust into bite-sized pieces and left them where her tongue could reach them. Much later, she heard him practicing his orations like songs. Like monks chanting in the distance, they were a comfort.

Rainbow settled onto the floor near the dog with her mind pleasantly buzzing through the endless variations of potential that required navigation in order to save the animal and make as few ripples in the fabric of reality as possible. She felt the boy's presence occasionally flit back to linger by the improvised bed. Each time he approached, Rainbow's focus wavered. His presence felt more solid than any human she had been around in eons, certainly more concentrated than it had been at the pizza shop. While most people's wishes skimmed up and off of them, begging for release and connection with others, his energies swirled tightly around him in currents of controlled aspiration, like strands of yarn making up a ball.

But the pizza kid moved off each time with only the renewed tendril of one wish escaping from the ball, that the dying animal be spared. After a few hours of work, Rainbow was certain she had successfully granted the wish for at least the next few weeks.

A longer delay of her passing would be more difficult and would have to wait until she knew more about the dog's potential owner and, therefore, her probable life.

Rainbow lifted her head from the dog and glanced around. The kid was gone. She stood stiffly and stretched. A bare bulb illuminated the cool, dingy garage casting odd shadows all around her, but a table lamp sat on the workbench along the back, its neck twisted and bent low over a book left open there. Rainbow turned a few open pages of *How to Make Friends and Influence People.*

The boy was focused, she had to give him that. She smiled to herself, recalling her time as a messenger and the influence she'd commanded through her sheer presence. Her rainbows had been the paths of many messages in the ancient era. Since the creation of these new communication devices though, she'd found significantly fewer wishes to fulfill about message carrying. Perhaps this boy could give her an outlet for that—her principal talent. He clearly wished to convey something important to many people. Since he was already working at it, granting his wishes would probably cause few wrinkles in the world; his achievements seemed bound to happen, and her magic would simply buoy that certainty, perhaps accelerate it a bit.

But what was the message he wanted to communicate? Rainbow flipped through the book, noting a few odd scribbles in the margins at points. It was in some sort of shorthand she couldn't make out and apparently written long enough ago that the intentions attached to their meaning had faded like those attached to the soggy offerings at the wall.

Finding no further clues in the book, she pulled her hand back. A fine gray coating remained on her fingertips where they had brushed the ink. She rubbed it on her jeans, but it stubbornly remained in place. She shook it a bit in aggravation and continued poking around the items on the workbench. There was little else nearby of any visible personal connection to the young man. Nothing that might help her learn his true aim. Some tools and what looked like a car part lay in a disheveled heap at one end and a locked filing box sat at the other with a handful of crumpled receipts strewn in front of it.

Rainbow turned and leaned against the workbench. She crossed her arms as she glanced around at the space again. Her fingers drummed on the sleeves of her white linen peasant top, leaving little smudges of dust as they did so. The garage was depressing.

Garages are, universally, the place of desires kept close at hand but not fulfilled. Within them, people store those items that, purchased on impulse, are sure to meet some as yet unmaterialized need and thus someday prove their usefulness. Garages are where projects are conceptualized and slaved over until they can be birthed to the world as bands, companies, or items of value. It's where people store their seasonal wishes of warmth, hope, and goodwill towards men. Garages are the home of wishes long since met and passed, but not yet ready to move on to new purposes and places.

This garage bothered her. Other than the book, it held none of the typical intent or hope for either things passed or yet to be. The items used to create the dog's makeshift shelter had the feel of cast-offs, discarded refuse never meant to be kept for either sentiment or purpose. They had been pulled from crisp, new boxes clearly marked for removal. Standing away from the old clothes, the only smell in the air was a tinge of antiseptic—none of the typical oil, dust, or paint.

She moved back toward the truck. If the guy had just moved in, then it was possible the unsettled feeling of the place was temporary. He likely kept more meaningful items close at hand, where he spent his days on the job.

Just as she laid her hand on the truck, she heard the interior door of the garage open. Rainbow froze, focusing on her veil. The boy did not pause in his strides over to the injured dog. He pulled the ragged coat back a bit, renewing the comforting rose scent on the air, and pet the dog gently.

As before, his desires were tightly controlled, wrapped around him in a protective bubble. But Rainbow noticed how the set of his shoulders relaxed as the dog thumped her tail happily against the side of the box. For a moment, his desires loosened, snaking out slightly from his body, allowing her to sense he wished to use this positive turn of events to his benefit. She tilted her head in confusion at the notion, but before she could follow the line of thought to understand how the dog's recovery could help him, the doorbell rang. The echoes of the chime snapped the boy out of his reverie and his desires back into an impenetrable ball.

The dog whimpered as he turned to head back inside. As he reached the threshold, the pizza kid turned back to the garage. His gaze passed over her standing by the truck and settled on the whining dog. A strong wish about the dog's continued health suddenly whipped out of his controlled bubble, causing Rainbow to gasp as it struck her like a physical slap in the face.

She knelt on one knee by the truck, certain her veil had slipped, but the repeated ring of the doorbell called the young man away. She stayed like that for a while, allowing the coolness of the concrete under her palms to ground her. The blinding demand of the boy's wish pulsed inside her closed eyes. She focused on it until she was able to push back against it, forcing it into narrow constraints she could easily meet without messing up reality.

A bead of sweat dripped off her nose, discoloring the light leather of her suede boot. Rainbow blinked, watching it spread. Once centered, she moved back over to the dog. Her heartbeat was strong and the internal organ damage was already mending from the wish-granting Rainbow had done earlier. She laid a shaky hand on the pup and let out a trickle of power, imbuing the poor girl with longevity, which she tied carefully to the young man's.

Rainbow settled back onto the floor and closed her eyes. The rose scent of the old clothes drifted around her and wrapped her in memories. She dreamed of herself, in her long white gown, connecting the sea and sky. She carried both water and fire and built bridges between the two for the people who, like her, sought to bring disparate people and places together. She brought messages of hope and peace from God and walked the entirety of the Earth in mere moments. Her memories shone and rippled behind her closed eyes.

Gradually, the scents in her memory shifted subtly to exotic spice, and she was walking beside Marco again as he looked for new trade goods. She smiled at the memory of his face, even as it aged, and his hair grayed in the theatre of her mind. Marco had wished to travel and have the skills to communicate with the new people of the Orient. She remembered vividly how his eyes crinkled when he spoke of how it would create a new class of people and an entirely new way of life. He'd dreamed big about his role in it, yet he'd never asked her to grant such wishes for him. Instead, Marco had given her the lamp that bound her to this plane—her charm. And she'd used the freedom gifted to her to stay by his side to the end of his life. Her fingers toyed with the charm on her bracelet again.

Rainbow ached with the desire to return to such happy times. With an effort, however, she wrenched her heart back to the present and pried her eyes open. She patted the dog, assured she had faithfully completed the wish, and climbed back to her feet. It was time to go.

She just needed to decide how best to leave without drawing attention. She walked around the truck, dismissing the main roll-up door out of hand. The noise would make it impossible to get away unseen. But a small back door, which likely opened out to the yard, would do fine. She strode over and turned the handle.

The knob stuck tight. Panic crawled up the edges of Rainbow's mind, not yet prominent enough to cloud her thinking but a definite presence nonetheless. There were no windows in the garage. No beams of light or prisms of glitter for her to ride out on.

The door to the house creaked open. Rainbow's head jerked up.

She met dark, steel eyes under graying curls. Eyes that she had seen before at the shrine with significantly less shrewdness. Without tears rolling down them, the sharp cheekbones clearly matched those of the young man now standing behind her in the doorway.

The man hustled past his mother and over to the dog, who sat up to greet him. Rainbow stuck fast to the spot, even as she realized her best chance of escape was rapidly closing again behind the woman. A wish that she remain where she was overwhelmed Rainbow's thoughts. Her heart rate quickened.

"How?" She heard the word escape her mouth without meaning to vocalize it. Tears threatened to well up as she continued looking at the woman before her. Neither she nor the young man answered, but the woman narrowed her eyes at Rainbow and scowled with distaste.

"Iris," the man used her old name. His back was still turned to her as he fussed with the puppy, but his motions now appeared intentional and constrained rather than those of the concerned and awkward pizza boy she'd seen before. When he turned, the tight ball of desires she'd sensed roiling inside him matched his perfectly controlled exterior.

"Obviously, we know what you are and how your nature compels you to grant the wishes of humans. But you are free and can choose the wishes you fulfill. Therefore, we had to devise a way to make our wishes the ones most like your own so that you would want to follow them. After all, you can't grant your own desires can you?"

Rainbow remained glued in place. Her chapped, strawberry

lips gaped slightly. The man snorted at her and continued, "How did you get so low as to resort to pet health as your main gimmick these days anyway? You have so much more power than that at hand. Why waste it like that?"

Before Rainbow followed the path of his statements to their logical conclusion about the cause of the dog's injury, the woman barked, "Do not give her an opportunity to speak until she is bound fully! She could yet evade you." To which the man threw back his head and laughed. It was a sinister laugh with so little joy or life to it that even in the mostly empty metal garage it died away without an echo.

"Why would she want to evade us, mother?" the man asked without moving his eyes from Rainbow's face. "Our plan would not have worked if she didn't want a reason to take back up her mantel of power. Her own wishes betray her. She wished for a task more substantial than pet ferrying to the afterlife. She wished to be remembered as the goddess of travel. She wished to be a powerful purveyor of messages again. And we have laid bare these wishes of hers. We have proven how unfilled they are. But…"

He paused dramatically, "We can fulfill them for her." He was looking deeply into her eyes as the rose scent wafted gently around the space. Between his hypnotic, confident cadence and the comfortable snuffling of the dog in the corner, Rainbow felt herself lulled back into happy memories. Perhaps he was right. She might stick with him for a bit and be like she once was.

A tug on her charm pulled her back to his eyes, which she hadn't realized had come so close during his talk. She looked down at her wrist, and her eyes widened. The tug had not been her own nervous habit, but the boy slipping her lamp into his hand. She hung her head in defeat.

Trapped by the delicate rose scent of nostalgia.

Author's Note: This piece was originally submitted as a part of Owl Canyon's Hackathon 2019. Portions of it (2 paragraphs) were provided by the publisher and are included in all the stories featured in <u>When the Ride Ends</u>.

BITTER HEART
By Marília Bonelli

Carved in ice or stone perhaps,

in disappointment for sure.

It's filled with questions that have no answers,

waiting solely to suffer again.

Knowing the ice will never melt

and the stone will never shatter,

it lives among its own lies.

And yet it hopes…

While cloaked in silent apathy,

it pleads for a love to reach it,

if any love could,

if any love would.

It latches onto a distant smile

and wise words fading in time,

and it hopes…

With bitterness or pure innocence,

it hopes that *never* may finally come to an end.

LOVERS OF STONE
By Stephen Woodfall

WHERE WAS CARYA HEADED at so late an hour?

Morto tugged his lambskin mantle tighter over his shoulders as he moved with stealth through the benighted woodland. A waxing moon dusted the edges of leaves with a ghostly glow. Near-invisible motes hung suspended in the warm, still air as if absorbing magic through the pale beams.

He followed, watching as Carya weaved her way through the trees. It had been betrayal and grief that drove Demeter into the underworld with only a torch in her hand. What secret drew his betrothed from her bedroom?

A sense of dread had stalked Morto like a stray mongrel since the day he bought the silk scarf. He waited for her at Demeter's Temple, but she never appeared. Her aloof behavior since only increased his fear and confusion.

Morto longed for the time when no secrets existed between them. A simpler time, when they spent summer afternoons racing hounds in the fields or reciting poems for each other in the dozing garden, sometimes inventing their own. They had sat side by side watching the dawn. And yet, the fondness they once shared faded as Carya began spending her days more and more often worshiping Demeter, always alone.

As their wedding day drew closer, his beautiful Carya had grown weary, her soft brown eyes losing their luster while dark crescents underlined her gaze. No longer did she sneak scraps to the hounds; no longer did she linger in the garden to give voice to poetry.

Could it be she was apprehensive about their childhood betrothal being fulfilled? Had she fallen into a melancholy over the memories of her noble father who, after being called upon by Menelaus to fight outside Troy's stout walls, had never returned?

Morto hurried his pace. All around, crickets and cicadas sang a strident chorus. He knew a spell that would deaden the sounds of his movement but decided the insects were noisy enough.

Beyond the darkling trees ahead, Carya's torch described a single wide circle through the air. A moment later, she set it upright, a flare that drowned out the surrounding moonlight with its wavering yellow glow.

At first, Morto sought to devote more time to dote on her, but walks in the garden and trips to the markets did little to lift her spirits. He bought gifts from the traders who sail to the east. He tried to rekindle their passion for the words and forms of poetry, but she only stared back at him without expression and asked to go pray to Demeter again.

Could Carya have taken a fancy to someone else? Had the

childhood love she had for him guttered and finally gone out? Or had it been rekindled by another? Someone she met in worship? If true, then her visits to the temple were a lie. A lie before the gods themselves. If she had played on Morto's faith and devotion and had been with another, he would never be able to forgive her.

He crept around a large boulder, and an opening in the trees came into view—an idyllic forest glade.

Shelves of moss-covered rock mounted in gentle steps from the grassy floor. Down them a thin brook tumbled, sounding out a light and playful music. The surrounding trees curved together overhead to form an arching green vault under which fireflies chased each other in flitting streaks.

The torch stood in a pile of rocks next to the brook, with Carya nearby, half of her form tinged with yellow light, the other half dissolving into shadow.

Morto cautiously crouched behind the twisted bole of a mighty oak tree, his suspicion rising. Why had Carya come to this spot? It was unlikely it had anything to do with Demeter, lady of harvest. This glade was too far from her fields and threshing floors, and the hour was wrong besides.

Minutes dragged by. Morto did not move. His guts writhed and roiled.

Just as his legs started to cramp, a figure appeared at the right side of the glade. The silhouette paused at the tree threshold for several heartbeats, then came striding out.

At the sight Morto's heart lost all energy; for a moment it ceased to beat.

It was a man. A *young* man.

Morto's eyes stung as an invisible weight descended upon him—a force sufficient to mold his soul into a new shape, distorted and painful.

The young man was called Telam. A lowlife imbiber and devotee of Dionysus. An empty-headed laugher and talker—a sudden loud noise followed up by nothing. Thick curly hair and a broad smile were his only assets in all the world.

Morto quaked as he watched the two come together, holding each other's hands and gazing into one another's eyes. His vision blurred crimson.

Time passed, but he did not know how much. A hushed voice reached him as he regained his senses. He raised his leaden head with effort and peered into the glade.

"…more than he appears," came Carya's husky whisper. "He studies ancient sorcery in secret, as I've told you before. It would be dangerous. I can't meet you again at night."

Telam's whisper was louder, less sibilant, and more urgent. "No longer in the afternoon. No longer at night. When else is there? I burn for you, my love, and I know you feel the same."

Carya slid her hand around Telam's back, pressing herself against his side as if for protection. "But my betrothed—"

"Is a dabbling, frittering fool," Telam finished. He leaned his face close to hers. "There is no need to worry about him or his ridiculous spells. Surely Apollo pays him no heed. But what of me?" He kissed her forehead softly. "In you, I discovered a love as true and clear as the sunrise. Having looked upon you, all else is now drear and drab. And should that sound like a curse from the Gods, it is one I would never choose to be free of."

She raised her voice, pleading. The sound tore at Morto's heart. "And so it is with me, too, Telam! Don't you see?"

Telam hugged her close. "We must go away soon, my love." He studied her face. "It must be soon."

Morto squeezed shut his red-filled eyes. Fury. It rushed through his body—a potent admixture of betrayal, envy, and humiliation. The shock of how quickly his heart changed from hot coals to cold ash surprised him. The weight of his rage threatened to push him into the dust and pin him there forever.

He would not bear the treachery alone.

A spark inside him flared to life at the thought—an ember of wrathful determination.

Morto was his father's son.

Like his father before him, Morto publicly feigned reverence for Apollo, but in secret gave his devotion wholly to Hecate. With the blessing of the goddess, he studied and practiced the sorcerous arts for years. He had even learned some of the forgotten lore of the ancients.

A plan formed swiftly in his mind. A fitting retribution. It would be as ghastly as it was ambitious, and once he thought of it, he could not set it aside.

Morto rose to his feet as if he were an automaton of Hephaestus' making. Surely Hera would prevent any other god from standing in the way of justice for a faithless lover.

Abandoning his need for stealth, Morto strode forward.

Carya and Telam were wrapped together in a deep kiss, immersed to the exclusion of all else. Morto's jaw tightened. She'd never kissed him like that, leaned into him when he'd been affectionate. Instead, she shied away, as if blushing. Another lie. So many lies.

Morto's lips curled with hatred. He slipped his fingers into the pouch he carried at his waist and took out a pinch of sand.

Only when he had come within a few paces did the lovers turn to look at him. But it was too late. Morto had summoned the proper balance of mind. Nothing on earth, nor upon Olympus, could stop him now. He lifted his hand, sifting sand between his fingers.

Carya broke free of her lover's embrace. Telam narrowed his eyes to gleaming slits and stepped in front of Carya as if to protect her.

Morto spread his arms, quivering palms forward.

"Morto! No!" called Carya. "No, wait. Please!"

Morto spoke in the ageless, grave tones of enchantment.

"Somnolescence!"

A deep silence fell upon the midnight glade, and the torchlight dimmed. Carya's eyelids fluttered a moment before she collapsed upon the grassy floor. Telam staggered backward, then fell on his back.

Far away, faint with distance, the sound of baying hounds seeped into the dark forest.

Morto set a flask of fresh water by a small container of lime. The two torches providing the only light in the dark cave had burned low, so he lit a third and placed it leaning in the shallow bowl of an empty stone brazier.

The blooming light fell in swaying dapples upon the still-sleeping figures of Carya and Telam. They were each bound tightly to a column with many more coils of rope than were necessary. Morto had arranged them so they faced one another across the width of the ancient underground temple.

All was nearly ready. He moved with a swaggering step though there were none to see and took a seat on the nearby bundle of hay to await the natural awakening of the betrayer and her lover.

The temple spread out before him. Its rudimentary columns stood in parallel lines running away on either side, the furthest only barely visible in the gloom at the edge of the torchlight. They supported a thick entablature atop their perimeter, cracked in places but otherwise whole. Small bits of the rubble of half an age were strewn across the floor, upon which four slab-shaped stone tables, or altars, were set.

The ancient site sat in a large cavern on Morto's ancestral property. His father had discovered it in his youth and told no one except Morto; it remained a secret place in which they could perform their rituals to Hecate without fear of discovery. Many of the runes and images led them to believe an early priesthood of Demeter had practiced their mysteries here. Morto guessed the place was eventually abandoned for the caves at Eleusis, but he could never know for certain.

Keeping Carya and Telam in view, he let his mind wander as the delicious taste of anticipation thrummed through him. Nevertheless, he sought to relax before he performed the final enchantment.

Sorcery was a delicate thing, and great sorceries more so. Long hard study was essential, but also practice and rigorous self-discipline. One also had to make proper obeisance to Hecate or no incantation of any kind would work. It was over a year since Morto failed to sacrifice two black ewes and honey on a particular night of the full moon. For a month afterward, he could not produce even the smallest of charms. It had been a painful lesson—never again had he failed the sacrifice.

A faint rustling interrupted his reverie. Carya's head lolled, and her draggling chestnut hair swayed before her face. Her coughs echoed through the cave.

Morto got to his feet and stepped over to Telam. Taking a fistful of the hair at the back of Telam's head, he yanked the man's head back and took a moment to glare into the bleary eyes as they opened and blinked.

Taking his time so as to savor the moment, Morto strolled to a point midway between his captives. "You were fools to think you could deceive me. To think you could deceive the gods. Fools!" He clenched and unclenched his fists as he spoke.

"Morto," Carya pleaded. "Let me explain. Please."

"Your words are lies." He faced his betrothed. "I loved you."

"And I you, Morto. You were my only friend."

"Friend, is it? I thought it something else. I thought we were as one, in our souls."

Her reddened eyes glistened in the light of the torches. "I was a child! I was in awe of you. I wanted to be like you. You were grown by then and knew what you wanted. And now that I'm grown, I've discovered my own wants too."

Morto paused. "You think this is about my wounded pride?"

"I'm sorry I hurt you."

Anger burned again. The feeling had come in waves from the moment he found the two lovers together. "You're right, I am hurt. I doted on you and cared for you. I shared my innermost thoughts. All I ever wanted was to share the rest of who I am with you as well."

Telam shouted, "You're a monster! We've all heard the rumors about your father. The dark sorcery."

"Rumors?" scoffed Morto. "You won't be relying on rumors any longer."

The horror in Telam's gaze was everything he could have hoped for.

"Morto, please!" Carya begged.

"You haven't offended me in the way you seem to think." Morto turned to retrieve the requisite components from the table nearby. "If it had simply been that you didn't love me anymore, I would have set you free."

Approaching Telam, the doomed follower of Dionysus, Morto daubed a trace of lime at the base of the man's neck, then poured some water on his head, into his curly hair. "You're a coward. You're both cowards. And liars."

He next treated Carya in a similar manner. "You lied before the gods. Made me part of your heresy. That I cannot forgive. Your punishment will appease those you have offended. From this time henceforth, you shall hold aloft physically a weight such as I shall bear in my heart."

Morto again placed himself midway between the two. The final moment had arrived; there would be no undoing such potent sorceries once performed.

"Until the end of time, you will gaze upon each other, and yet remain ever apart. You will feel nothing other than the unceasing burden of this forgotten temple."

Girding himself, Morto raised his arms, coaxing into being the necessary inner balance. He lidded his eyes lightly and gave voice to the sonorous words for binding, melding, and longevity. The cadences swelled and filled the great underground space with multitudes of sharp reverberations.

With all his strength, he shouted the last two words of the enchantment, loud and clear.

"*Caryatid! Telamon!*"

Carya squeezed shut her eyes while Telam strained against his bindings. A rumbling, cracking issued from some distant place, from deeper within the earth. The cavern shuddered. Dust sifted down to the temple floor.

Morto went down on one knee, enraptured by the splendor of it all, his eyes locked on Carya's face.

The sorcerous transition was prolonged, lasting several minutes. Carya's form was pressed hard against the pillar she was tied to by an unseen force. Her lips parted, then froze. The rosiness on her cheeks faded as her staring, imploring eyes lost their moisture. She sank into the stone as her skin and clothing and hair all took on an ashen hue. The length of column behind her lost much of its mass and shaped itself to her frame even as she sunk further into it.

The distant rumble receded. The cavern grew still, and the dust settled.

It was done. Carya and the column were one and the same. The circular base tapered sharply to form her feet, and then flared out again above her head, resuming its original shape.

Opposite her, Telam's lying lips and curling hair were frozen for all time.

Morto collapsed to the floor. In moments, darkness took him.

Holding his torch high, Maerlo's servant stepped out of the cave entrance.

"It opens out into a large cavern, sir," he said.

"A cavern?" said Maerlo. "Is that so?"

The old man nodded.

Maerlo sighed and stared out at the horizon while a light wind played across the tops of the nearby trees. It was an hour shy of noon. There was still much to be done and they were nearly two miles from the manse.

He had no wish to sell off parcels of the ancestral land before learning more about it first. For all he knew, this cave might be the place his eccentric great-great-grand uncle Morto was reputed to have practiced his grandest sorceries.

"Right," he said. "We'd better check it out then."

Maerlo followed his servant through the entrance. The passage descended steadily, and the air became damper and mustier the further they went. The way wound around two gentle curves before opening into a great underground space.

The servant lit a second torch from his own and handed it to Maerlo. They moved forward, peering into the outer limit of their collective light.

Ahead, a structure loomed into view—an ancient temple of rudimentary design.

As they drew nearer, Maerlo beheld it was partially collapsed. Beyond and between the columns in front of them, others were leaning or fallen and crumbled. Little of the entablature remained aloft; most of it lay in pieces large and small.

Maerlo and his servant picked their way through the rubble, looking for anything of interest. Rounding a huge chunk of fallen stone, something caught Maerlo's eye. A variation in the otherwise unadorned stonework of the old temple. Lifting his torch, he stepped closer.

One of the fallen pillars had been shaped into a human form, a man. The dimensions and detail were far more realistic than Maerlo had ever seen in a carving before. It made no sense, in light of how the rest of the temple was so crudely wrought.

Squinting, he stepped nearer. He rubbed his eyes and looked

again.

It should not be.

There were two of the human-shaped columns, a man and a woman, lying in the rubble of the structure they once held. Their faces were turned toward each other, as close together as they could be.

AN UNFAMILIAR FEELING
By Marília Bonelli

LAUGHTER DRIFTED INTO THE shadows of Luke's hiding place, sneaking between the trees like tendrils of some long-forgotten childhood memory. Everyone was headed home.

Perhaps there would be a warm meal waiting for them, surrounded by smiling faces. He could almost imagine it, conjuring up pieces of dreams that were all but gone now.

Self-consciously, Luke straightened his shirt, pressing his hand against his chest. The various valleys that formed his scars were a sobering reminder of his place in this world. He couldn't help trace a few letters through the thin fabric—*forfeit*.

Had he been expected to forfeit hope along with his life?

He pulled his hand away, resting a clenched fist on a nearby tree. Anya hated when his thoughts went down that path. She could always see it in his eyes, like she had that morning.

She'd been laughing as she told him that her parents would be coming for the New Year. Here in Allea, the New Year was celebrated by going home and exchanging gifts with those you cherished.

At the temple in Tretion, where he'd been trapped for most of his life, the end of the year festival was a time of giving thanks for life's blessings. Having been deprived of such blessings, he'd never had any use for it. It felt bitter at best.

"Come home with me," Anya had asked that morning, her lingering kiss still fresh on his lips.

He'd wanted so much to say yes, but the word stuck in his throat, held captive by a fear that not even the monster-filled forest he currently resided in could elicit from him.

His hand returned to his chest, following the shape of his scars with morbid precision—*forfeits his life*. But his life was no longer forfeit. And it wasn't as if he'd never stepped outside the forest since. He could do it for Anya, couldn't he?

She was, after all, the only good thing his cursed existence had brought him—whether by a trick of fate or wretched coincidence. A capricious fortune, at least, to have formed such a pair: a would-be murder victim and the man who killed her attacker.

Before his finger could absently trace the crime he'd been convicted of, the familiar sound of boots against the hard ground stopped him cold.

Allean enforcers.

He sank back further into the protective shadows of the surrounding trees, but his eyes could not look away. He tried to suppress the instinctive dread that came with their presence—they'd been the ones used by the temple to torture and terrify him.

His fingernails dug into the rough bark. Everywhere was filled with ghosts.

He checked behind him, but his horse was still well-hidden, her dark coat merging naturally with the shade.

Luke readjusted his shirt, making sure to hide the scars. He just had to wait until the enforcers were further away, and he could go. The rational part of his brain understood that the patrol would not have a reason to detain him now that he was considered free. They wouldn't even recognize him as a criminal. Not unless—

A flash of white emerged from within their ranks.

Luke hid himself behind a tree automatically. Why would they have a stain reader—someone capable of detecting the lingering trace of death—out here on patrol? Or were they escorting him to the border?

Never mind his actual crime, Luke definitely had a stain now.

He was a killer. The identity of the victim did not alter that fact.

It took him longer than he expected to reacquire a semblance of calm. By then, the patrol and the stain reader were long gone. It was a while longer before he managed to dispel the darkness in his thoughts. Telling himself he no longer had a reason to be afraid was of little use.

Fireworks sounded, a brief display signaling the start of the festivities on the other side of town. The horse nudged him gently, and Luke patted her flank. "Not yet, still too many people around."

It would be easier to sneak out of the woods, unseen, after dark. And more time would put more distance between him and the stain reader—even if just for his peace of mind.

Rustling signaled movement behind him. Luke turned, meeting the icy blue eyes and sharp fangs of a shadow wolf. A creature of this forest, Ammyla also did not belong in the world outside. But unlike him, the forest truly was her home.

"Don't look at me like that."

The large predator returned his glare. She made no move to leave, as if she could feel his reluctance.

"I'm going... You should go back before you give someone a heart attack."

Never mind seeing a man emerge from this cursed forest— and on horseback, no less—the sight of a shadow wolf so close to the city would surely cause a completely different level of panic. "Probably not a good start to anyone's year." He patted the wolf's head.

Howls rose in the distance. Ammyla did not respond, but her ears twitched, making her look almost cute. Maybe a similar phenomenon affected Anya, his ghosts taunted. Luke wasn't afraid of Ammyla—she'd fed him and protected him—and Anya, likely for similar reasons, was unafraid of him. Neither would see the killer staring right at them as long as the thing was warm, cuddly, and reasonably well-behaved.

He found himself hesitating, but hadn't Anya asked him to come?

Ammyla whined. He offered her a feeble smile, bending to wrap his arms around her neck. The smell of last night's campfire still persisted on her coarse fur. "Go on. I'll find you later."

With a parting huff, Ammyla soundlessly vanished back into the darkness.

The crowds thinned as sunlight changed to warmer shades of orange and red. Taking advantage of a lull in the unwanted presence of people, Luke spurred Bo out of hiding. Hoofbeats echoed off the brick houses as they hurried along. The sound was oddly satisfying, though it brought more than one curious face to a window.

His hands clutched the reigns, trying not to return their stares as cold sweat formed on his back.

The echoes multiplied and became mismatched. Confused, he brought Bo to a stop. Still, the echoes continued. Rounding a corner and stepping into a ray of light came a horse that looked like it had been born from the fading sun. Recognizing the horse and its dark-haired rider, Luke urged Bo into a run.

Anya practically threw herself off the horse when Remi came to a stop. Luke had barely dismounted before she hurled herself into his arms.

"Why are you here?" Concern momentarily overpowered the joy that came with her embrace. "Did something happen? Your parents—"

"I left them a note."

"Then what—"

"I was afraid you wouldn't come," she said into his shoulder. When she released him, a smile flickered on her lips. "I wouldn't be able to do this properly…"

She pulled out a small box from her pocket. Luke hadn't seen her that embarrassed since they met, when she clung to him out of fear after being dragged into the badlands. "I know it's not an actual home, but maybe someday it can be."

Inside the box was a key to her place, complete with a little wolf key chain that looked remarkably like Ammyla.

"For now, if you want, you can think of it as an anchor... or a harbor, I guess." Her voice trembled slightly, words coming faster as nervousness peeked through. "A place where you can feel comfortable outside the badlands."

Could he? Could he really? Even now, his mind was aware of the passing stares.

Anya splayed a hand on his chest, over the scars that had once terrified her. "It's just fear. Isn't it?"

Luke placed a hand over hers, feeling the pounding of his own heart. Hadn't he said those words to her before, when they entered the badlands?

"I'm right here with you," she said.

A chuckle escaped him. Those were definitely his words. He squeezed her hand, remembering what she'd asked him then. "Does the fear go away?"

"Someday," she whispered, deviating from their script.

Luke held the key like a precious treasure.

He'd failed miserably at trying to find something worthy of being gifted to her.

"I have nothing to give you but my heart," he said, the truth escaping of its own accord. "And that's already yours."

Anya's eyes widened, her hand almost slipping from

underneath his.

Could she not know?

"Anya…" Luke entwined their fingers, pressing her hand gently over the pounding in his chest as he held her gaze. "I love you."

Her entire face lit up; her eyes shone.

"Will you come with me then, just a little further?" She leaned into him, a bit of mischief as she once again borrowed his words.

Luke captured her lips in a greedy kiss, heart and mind struggling with whether to hold her close or release her. But her arms enveloped him, pulling him closer, deepening the kiss.

He wouldn't—couldn't—let go.

"Where do you want to go?" he asked, willing to follow her anywhere, even in the midst of that crowded city.

She smiled, the setting sun lighting up her storm-filled eyes. "I'll go wherever you go."

He tightened his embrace, burying his face in the crook of her neck. When he breathed in, her warmth spread through every cold, dark corner of his being.

It really didn't matter where they went… *she* was his home.

JUST GEESE
By V. George

WHEN WILL CAME HOME, the flowers were already in a vase on the dining table. He poured four fingers of bourbon and planted himself there, his back to the hall. By the time Dacia's keys rattled at the front door, the world was fuzzy, and the top of his tongue smoldered with the whiskey.

Dacia stepped in, and the magenta hues of the sunset burned in her bangs.

"What are you doing?" she asked.

"That's not where the flowers belong."

"Well, they were wilting on the table. They'll last longer this way."

"I didn't need them to last longer. I needed to count their leaves."

Dacia's dark eyes went wide. Her lips, red at just the edges, folded in a tight line.

"You cut the leaves, didn't you? So they could fit in that narrow vase?"

"They're still in the trash can, they're not totally gone. I can lay them out for—"

"And I suppose you can tell me which flower correlated with which plot?" Will asked. Dacia huffed and strode into the adjoining kitchen. From his seat at the table, Will heard the slap of her purse hitting the counter and the rattle of the trash bag. He raised his voice. "I suppose that these ironweed… or maybe these goldenrods here were in the shaded half of the field, but that would be guessing. Not science."

"You study flowers, not leaves," Dacia snapped as she clicked back into the room empty-handed.

"That's right, I *study* them. I'm a botanist. Not…" he waved his glass at the bouquet, "not a florist."

Dacia put her hands on the table and sighed. "You've been smoking."

Indeed, when Will came home, he found the old ashtray with the whiskey, a timeless pair. Now it sat in front of him, home to two crushed butts.

"You said you quit back in March."

"It's good for you," Will joked.

"I thought you were the scientist." Before Will could protest, she snatched up the ash tray and went back to the kitchen. If the leaves weren't ruined before, now they were covered in lukewarm ashes.

She returned without the ashtray. Will groaned. She'd thrown the whole thing out.

"I can't believe you're already toasted."

"It's a Friday night." But hadn't she said something similar yesterday, or perhaps the evening before?

"It is, and I *wanted* to go out and get some dinner. That's why I put the flowers in there. To preserve them for the weekend so you'd take a damn night off."

Will picked at the nicks in the table with his flat, bitten nails. The wood underneath was lighter than the stain, perhaps some cheap maple. Dacia was waiting for Will to look at her, or maybe thank her for her thoughtfulness, and he knew it. She had a way of staring, head tilted and eyes wide, that used to make him heavy with guilt. But now he just wanted another cigarette. He grazed his hand over his pocket, over the glossy edge of the pack.

"We're going. Just let me put on my lipstick."

And that was how Dacia solved things, all pretty. The flowers in a vase, lipstick fresh on her face. Dinner out sounded like as good a place as any to order a beer and ignore her, so Will didn't wait. He marched straight to the car while she ducked into the half-bath. Her protests were muffled when the front door shut behind him.

She caught up and threw his door open just as he was turning the ignition in his shitty Ford Focus. "Oh, no you don't. You've been drinking."

He scrunched his nose at her. "Just a glass, to take the edge off." It wasn't entirely a lie, considering he had drunk from the same glass.

She closed his door, but Will didn't miss the roll of her eyes as she came around to the passenger side. She buckled in with more force than necessary.

As they drove, Will's nose stayed scrunched. The car smelled like the acid of a cut lawn. As though the weeds he'd been hauling home had stained the very seats. He'd wrap them in more newspapers next time and pray the smell went away. He really wanted a cigarette, if only to burn the smell out of his nose.

"You're swerving." Dacia clung to the clothes hanger above. "You're drunk."

Will didn't have a retort for that, because he was. "You know what I think," he said instead. "I think you just want real fucking flowers."

Dacia was quiet, as though she had the audacity to consider this. As though they both weren't sick and tired of flowers. "You know what? That would be nice."

"Are you serious?"

"Watch the road, Will."

"Really now? Flowers? What a nice gesture that would be! Date a botanist and get flowers every day! Is that what you thought?"

"I thought I dated a botanist, but I married an asshole."

"Jesus Chr—"

Will put his hand in his pocket and found the pack.

"What are you even doing?"

"What does it look like I'm doing?" He waved the crumpled box at Dacia. "I'm stressed, I'm having a cigarette."

"Will! Watch the road!"

He tilted back into his lane. "I'm watching," he said, laughing a bit. The way someone does to defuse awkwardness.

Dacia was not convinced. "Will, pull over!"

Will raised the lighter to his cigarette and flicked his thumb over the wheel only once before the Ford sailed over the hill. The car and its rusted shocks landed like a brick on the hillside. Will, his lighter, and his cigarette all slapped the roof with the crack of teeth.

In the distance, behind the ringing, Dacia screamed. The car sailed down, down the hill towards the river. Slaughterhouse Hill, Will recognized with the dimmer part of his concussed brain. He hadn't been here since he was a child.

As Dacia's screams curdled, the blood settled in the folds of the front of Will's brain, where the most bitter of memories were tucked away. And so, as the Ford hurtled down, Will didn't remember his cigarette or his anger or Dacia. He didn't remember when he threw away that scrapbook of mislabeled tree leaves she gave him, which he once found so endearing. He didn't remember when he first noticed the disarming optimism beneath her smile or when it began to drain him.

The good memories were buried too deep in the recesses of his childhood. And so, he didn't remember the leather encyclopedias that went only to 'L'. Or how he used to lay belly-bare on sticky linoleum and memorize the magical drawings of amphibians, birds, fishes, and flowers. How he wished he could trace the glossy outlines of reptiles and mammals. He didn't remember flipping stones in the creek to catch crawdads, praying for the rare frog or salamander to categorize. Or how his Ma yelled at him when he used her sewing pins to fix moths to his wall. To study them. He didn't remember Ma at all, even though he had promised himself he would never forget her scent. Like licorice.

Instead, he remembered cold, the light scratch of his jacket over itself. His little sister skipping down Slaughterhouse Hill with the back of her puffy coat to him. A bag of white bread swung in her hand with each bouncing step.

"Ma says breaths are white when it's cold 'cuz they make our clouds up in heaven," she said. Will caught a glimpse of her face, like a fog, like a dream. "That's why Da smokes all year."

This was that slip of time after their parents separated, but before the encyclopedias didn't fit in Ma's double-wide.

"That's not how it works," Will heard himself say.

"Well, how does it?"

Will had read about condensation in a science magazine. But he'd never said the word out loud before. It was long and cluttered where it sat on the tip of his tongue. He swallowed and said nothing.

"Ma says the more you breathe the bigger your cloud in heaven gets."

And then there was the river, the green water lapping at the toes of her butterfly boots. She blew out and out. Geese, black-billed and crass, glided in the fogged distance.

"G-*whooooooo*-ses." A huge cloud drifted from her.

"No, it's '*geese*'. Not '*gooses*'," Will said. The bile of inevitability sat heavy on his tongue. He threw a slice of bread on the river.

"G-*heeeeeeee*-ses." The cloud was smaller. "It's not the same."

"That's because it's geese. Just geese."

The great gray birds had finally noticed and were approaching now. They stretched out their long, black necks, beaks to the sky.

Their pink tongues flared and they laughed and they laughed.

"G-*heeeeeeese*," she blew out. "Just g-*heeeeeeeese*."

KOROVA
By L. H. Adamkiewicz

WHEN WE LEFT THE men's prison camp, we had next to nothing. The packs we stole had no GPS, no screenshots of troop movements, not even a confiscated smartphone. We were walking through a vast wilderness with just an old Iditarod map and a compass that somehow hadn't frozen solid yet. White Mountain was at least two days' walk away, but we weren't expecting a hard trip.

Then the storm hit.

I hadn't lived in Alaska long, but even by Alaskan standards, the weather was absolutely wretched. An ice storm had been sitting on us for days. Every minute brought a new burst of freezing cold wind off the Bering Sea, flinging sharp flecks of ice. Most of the ice bounced off of my coat, but stray shards found their way into the crease between my outer jacket and my ushanka with needle-like pinches. I was wearing three substantial layers, yet I'd never been colder in my life. At least we weren't crawling through multiple feet of snow while battling sub-zero temperatures.

Our packs seemed to get heavier every day. My bag contained two sleeping bags and some fire starter sticks, but it felt like I was carrying a boat anchor. I only hoped they were enough to keep us from freezing to death before we reached the beachhead. Blondie got off easy with the map and compass, wire-cutters, a knife too dull to cut through buttered bread, and I was certain, the last of our rations. Yet, each time I asked about them, my tall Russian acquaintance changed the subject. Blondie hadn't looked me in the eye for a few hours now—strange behavior for a man who seemed to pride himself on being able to make anyone feel at ease.

My stomach growled loudly enough to hear over the howling wind. It had been making noises for days. I wondered how long had it taken that hippie guy who died in the van to starve after he was too weak to get up and eat?

The sun was low in the wind-swept sky when I tripped.

"You're alright?" I could hear a touch of sympathy and worry in Blondie's voice.

"Yeah, fine," I spat. "One sec." I wanted to ask him to come a little closer if he was that concerned. Maybe take a real close look at my fist. But I stopped myself. Riling someone up in the middle of an ice storm just didn't seem like the best move.

I dug my toe into the snow to see what had tripped me. The beige rock had been rounded into roly-poly waves by the sheer force of constant wind from the coast. It was a good size—big enough to do some damage, light enough that I could carry it with me.

I made sure that Blondie wasn't watching me. Then I slipped the ice-cold rock into the pocket of my enormous outer coat.

I should have known that things were going to get ugly after I met Gunderson at the saloon last August.

"Jesus," Gunderson said, pointing at the ancient box TV hung up over the bar. "I can't believe it. Are you seeing this?"

I'd been trying to avoid the news. There was only so much I could take of the racist, sexist, moronic douche-nozzle our fellow citizens had seen fit to put into high office.

"Jesus," Gunderson said again. "He might as well give the Russians the White House security codes!"

"Which Russians are those?" I asked, trying to force my features into the picture of wide-eyed innocence.

Gunderson didn't take the bait, but he grinned as he shook his head. "Every tinpot dictator on the globe has to be laughing at us right now."

I looked around the saloon before I spoke. Alaska is a deep red state, and we couldn't start making enemies now. The fact that Gunderson and I were opening Nome's first big-box store was only going to get us so far. "That's why my cousin Misha loves him. Did you order already?"

"Yeah, the waitress said my burger and rings will be up in fifteen." Gunderson was about to take a sip of his beer when he stopped. "Wait, can you eat anything here?"

Most people saw my short, three-hundred-pound frame and thought I needed to eat a damn salad already. I blame it on Mom coming from good Russian stock. I was born so big that Mom needed a C-section. Being fat enough to need medical assistance at birth would have fazed some people. Not my Russian grandparents. They loved it. It almost made up for the fact that Mom had married a corn-fed American boy.

They were all certain I was going to be a weightlifter. For years, they cooed over me and my many rolls. *What a good strong boy! A blessing to your family!* But it was fat. And no matter what anyone did, over the last thirty-five years, I stayed fat.

Fat little legs, fat little arms, fat little belly.

Fat. Fat. Fat. Fat. Fat.

Most people just saw the fat when they looked at me. It had been hell in grade school. But Gunderson had helped me get my nutritionist's meals delivered up here. He was also one of the few people I knew who could take a joke.

"You've heard me complain about every quinoa grain I've eaten for the past six months, and you think I need help watching my weight?"

"Uff da, still as charming as a beauty queen, aren't you?" Gunderson said.

"I've got cheat days," I promised him. "Don't you worry about me."

Thankfully, Gunderson unwound a little at that.

"Isn't Misha your douchebag cousin?"

When we drank, Gunderson sometimes blew off steam about

his beautiful wife, three kids, and the troubles they had moving here from Minnesota. And I—single bachelor that I was—complained about the asshole relatives I'd left behind. I missed my family back in the lower forty-eight sometimes, but not Misha. That asshole was always trying to mess with me, trying to fire me up so he could beat me down.

When we were kids, the beatdowns were literal. I kicked his ass every time, and he always said it was a fluke because he couldn't have lost to a fat baby. The rest of the family would stand around, holding plates full of pelmeni and paprika-laced potato salad, watching Misha attack me. They thought it was hilarious.

"Yeah, that's him. You know that asshole swore he would make me his *korova*?"

I was twelve. We'd been fighting in my grandma's backyard in the Nebraska summer heat. I had nailed Misha with a haymaker, and his nose was bleeding. I told Misha in his stained wife-beater that I hoped the next time he got arrested—he was on juvenile probation for beating up his girlfriend and torturing her cat—the KGB would send him to starve to death in Siberia.

Misha hadn't liked that. *I'll take you with me! I'll make you my korova!*

The adults, all of whom had been more than happy to sit around and watch us kick the crap out of each other, hissed and gasped at the word. Misha was pulled off to the side, and I was taken into the house. They never let us fight again.

"What's a *korova*?" Gunderson asked.

"Trust me," I said, my eyes fixed on the ancient TV, "you don't want to know."

Later that night, when we found the odd little outcropping of rocks by the side of the mountain, Blondie's face lit up. I couldn't help but smile along with him.

"This proves the Iditarod map is still good, yes? The White Mountain checkpoint is close. Maybe two more days' journey. This is good news!"

It was the kind of pep talk that any good leader would give their team. Point out the positive and keep everyone focused on the end goal. Not for the first time, I wondered what the hell Blondie had done before he ended up here. He wouldn't talk about his past. He had a thousand ways of charmingly not answering the question while redirecting your attention elsewhere. I'd asked him if he had led some kind of group. Maybe he had been with a faction of anti-government crusaders before being tapped by the Russian military or a newly appointed leader of a group of soldiers. He always brushed off my questions with an airy, accented, *It is possible.*

The only time I got an actual response was when I'd asked if he was a spy. His eyes flashed with a splinter of cold meanness I didn't realize he possessed. He'd seen the panic on my face and shrugged, unbothered.

All Russians spy on one another. If you know things, you will survive.

He had said it so matter-of-fact at the time. A pure statement, no guilt or remorse. He did what he had to do, and that was it.

Yet, he didn't look like a hardened man as he smiled at the Iditarod map spread out on the snowy earth. He looked like a kid determined to build a snow fort, poring over the plans he had carefully sketched in crayon.

"Are you not pleased?" he asked me, happily brushing the falling snowflakes off of the crinkled plastic surface.

"I'm still not sure how we're going to survive all of this."

"It is only another day or two. We can both handle the cold. We are both strong like ox. Come, see."

He gestured for me to come closer and look at the map. The wind was blowing in from the south, harder now.

To see what he was pointing at, I'd have to turn my back to him.

I spotted a dead shrub at the base of the mountain and decided to lie like a cheap rug. "Let's start a fire first. We'll need to melt some snow if we've got two days of travel ahead."

"Come closer, my friend. You could see perfectly with my flashlight."

I wanted to ask him how stupid he thought I was. I forced myself to chuckle instead.

"Fire first. Even an ox needs water."

It happened the day before the grand opening.

The only battle I expected to have that day was with Johnson—

who had gotten in the nasty habit of acting like he owned the place. I could usually get the more social climbing employees in line with some well-timed comments about their obvious personal issues. But Johnson was too stupid for any of my normal observations to find their mark. He'd been a pain in my ass since we started the project, and he seemed to relish undermining my authority.

The walk-through wasn't even on the official schedule for that day. Gunderson and I were just taking the staff and vendors through the store one last time. It was near the end of the day, so a couple of people ended up bringing their families. Not our typical procedure, but we signed off on it. It was winter in Nome, after all. There wasn't exactly a lot more going on.

We weren't even doing anything, really, when the store was hit. The employees were standing around talking about nothing in particular. Gunderson was holding his fussy newborn baby girl. The wives were keeping an eye on the older kids as they raced up and down the aisles.

When I first saw the waves of men in Russian camo pouring through the aisles, I thought it was a flash mob. A prank. Hell, for a second, I wondered if I had fallen asleep and was hallucinating.

Then I felt the cold muzzle of a huge gun dig into my back.

The soldiers immediately separated the men from the women and children. They marched us outside at gunpoint and lined us up on the sidewalk. There were huge trucks with barred passenger compartments idling in the parking lot.

That's when it hit me that this was bigger than some local militia or sick prank. They had battle vehicles. They arrived ready to transport prisoners.

The men were loaded and secured first. As we pulled away, I saw a young soldier pull Mrs. Gunderson and the now-screaming baby out of the line. The soldier ripped the baby girl out of her shaking hands and tossed her on the ground.

I turned my head away, but I still heard the shot.

For a moment I went numb with shock.

Then I realized I knew what they were saying.

Though it had been years since I spoke Russian, I started catching a few stray words from the guard in the passenger seat. I racked my brain to try and figure out what they were saying. *Idiot... going to... prison*?

As the armored car shook on the uneven roads, his buddy said something I didn't quite catch, but one word was clear. "Tiše." *Be quiet.*

"W-what are they saying?" Gunderson asked me, his voice shaking.

"Hell if I know."

Gunderson knew I was Russian. Knew that in spite of my very American last name, I spoke Russian.

He also knew enough to shut up.

"Did you ever do time in Siberia?" I held my hands in front of the small fire to dry my mittens.

"Why do you ask?" Blondie said.

"You treat imprisonment as an inconvenience, and you're strolling through dogsled country like most people walk through a park. I just made an assumption. Am I right?"

"My past career took me many places. Siberia was one of those places."

"You're not going to talk about what you were doing before all this, are you? You're still going to pretend that you were quietly sitting in a room eating borscht-flavored chips for the last ten years of your life?"

He gave the same airy wave that made me laugh back in the camps. "I did what I had to do."

I smiled as if I didn't care. "Well, whatever you did, I'm glad you did it. I don't know how I could have gotten this far without you. I'm not exactly an outdoorsy guy. All I remember from Boy Scouts is how to use a compass."

"But that has been very handy, yes?" Blondie nodded toward my pack. "And you've been carrying half of our equipment. Strong like an ox!"

I was starting to hate that phrase. I wasn't an ox. An ox could fight back if you tried to lead it somewhere it didn't want to go.

I wasn't in the same fighting shape I was in when I last tried to take down Misha. My trainers and nutritionists had spent years focusing on cardio and endurance exercises in an attempt to peel the weight off. Those years of training sessions had taught me to ignore my hunger and focus on long-distance aerobic goals. Granted, those skills were definitely paying off now. But I wasn't exactly in the best shape to fight back against an attacker.

Especially after coming this far. With little sleep, and less food.

"I just wish we'd managed to get a few more rations," I grumbled. "Slogging through this snow and ice against this goddamned wind is brutal. We might die of hunger before we get to White Mountain."

"We have enough food to get to White Mountain," Blondie told me. "I know this."

His smile was kind. His eyes were sharp.

I felt a shiver of ice race up my spine.

I learned real quick that you never wake up optimistic in a prison camp—if you could even call it that.

We were forced into a little containment area that was just a circle of tents and pop-up shelters, surrounded by rings of barbed wire, all-terrain prisoner transports, and overly armed guards. The whole thing felt as ridiculous as a battalion guarding a discount pup tent.

They put us to work the next day doing the tough jobs, the mindless jobs. With the temperatures getting down to -10°F most days and mountains of snow appearing overnight, there was always something to do. Clearing snow. Breaking ice. Hauling water when the pumps froze solid in the middle of the night.

But as the days racked up and I kept surviving, I started to notice some things.

The guards were careless when they spoke in front of us.

Understandable, since the stereotype of Americans only knowing basic English exists for a reason. As more and more Russian came back to me, I listened to them talk and realized what was happening.

This was Phase One of an invasion—an invasion, that, after the second month, was not going as well as expected. U.S. troops were coming down from Utqiagvik, Alaska, near the North Pole. And there was a resistance force island-hopping through the Aleutians as best they could in the Alaskan winter. Turns out that even the most incompetent, racist asshole of a president could only delay a military response for so long.

The Russian government had quickly written their invasion off as a failure. In a bid to keep power on the world stage, they dismissed the soldiers as a splinter group and stopped sending supplies.

Our meager food rations were cut in half overnight.

Waves of biting hunger became just another constant in the camp. Each day, I knew that the sky would be blue, the work would be hard, and I would get so hungry I'd start wondering what my own arm would taste like. I had never liked that wobbling bob of skin under my arms anyway. If I could slice it off without bleeding to death, I was sure I could fry it up and hork it down before the guards got wise. I just wanted a slice of meat, real meat, one more time before I died.

And each time the urge to mutilate myself came over me, it made me remember the korova.

One day, Gunderson and I were at the back of a team

returning from a road clearing job. The guards behind us were distracted, nervously discussing the latest US troop movements as we trudged back on the freshly cleared road. We had just gotten a new shipment of prisoners in. Defectors and deserters from the Russian army. I had seen one of them trying to talk to Gunderson earlier. So, I quietly asked Gunderson if anyone had offered to help him escape.

"Like as a joke?" he asked.

"No. For real. Has anyone come to you and asked you to join them in escaping the camps?"

"Hell no. I haven't been that lucky." Gunderson said.

When I let out a deep sigh of relief, he looked at me suspiciously.

"What? Should I know something?"

I carefully looked at the guards behind us. They had been our regular watchdogs for months. The only English they seemed to understand was *bathroom*, *yes*, and *no*. Like the rest of our captors, they didn't exactly look like the best the Russian army had to offer, but now wasn't the time to start testing their hidden depths.

"Look, we can't say it because they might recognize the word, but do you remember the weird term I mentioned? When we were talking about my douchebag cousin at the bar? The word that started with a K that I didn't want to talk about?"

Gunderson waited until the guards turned to each other, arguing over something, and then mouthed the word back to me. *Korova?*

"That's it. Look, I didn't want to ruin your burger back then, but it's something you should look out for."

"What is it?"

"Well, the word itself means 'cow', but the way my cousin used it, it means something else. Or it could mean something else. Honestly, it might just be an urban legend. But… well…"

"What does it mean when someone wants to turn you into a cow?"

"Look, it used to be that if you did something unforgivable, you would be sent to a camp in Siberia. Those camps were bitterly cold, had little food and water, and a schedule designed to work you to death in months. Win-win, really. Your work would benefit the state, and in time you'd no longer be a problem."

"So exactly what we're doing."

"More or less. That's why you had to get creative if you wanted to escape. You had a better chance at survival if you came into the camps with some physical labor under your belt, but not every prisoner was so lucky. Some of the prisoners were bureaucrats, accountants. Mom used to call them soft men."

"I take it that the soft men didn't last long?"

"That's why they were desperate to get out. The story goes that if a tougher prisoner wanted to escape, they'd make friends with one of the soft men. They'd do some of the soft man's labor, share their meager rations, and fill the soft man's head with stories of an upcoming escape. Eventually, the two men would escape together. But only the tougher prisoner would ever make it back to civilization."

"Why would the tougher prisoner drag the soft guy along, if he was just going to die along the way?"

"Because there's a lot of calories in a human cadaver."

Gunderson just looked at me.

"Are you serious?"

"You're not going to pick up a cow and carry it to the slaughterhouse when it's strong enough to walk there on its own. The real escapee would lead 'the cow' halfway to safety. Then when 'the cow' was at his weakest, he'd kill him, eat him, and use the extra calories to make it to civilization. Or so the legend goes."

"Come on, man. Even if... look, you'd need a fire—a big fire—if you even wanted to attempt something like that."

"Would you?"

The dawning horror on Gunderson's face was the same mine must have worn when Mom first told me the tale. Because no. No, you wouldn't. Starving people aren't that picky.

I grabbed his arm and forced him to keep walking.

"But it's just a rumor, right? An urban legend?"

"I don't know. I honestly don't. When Mom first told me about it, I went to libraries, Google, wherever I could to prove that it was just a sick fairy tale. I never found enough evidence to prove or disprove anything. But Rus—" I stopped myself, remembering the guards. "But people from *that country* have found ways to survive situations far worse than the one we're in right now. Even when escape is impossible."

And for Gunderson, it turned out, escape was impossible.

A few nights later, Johnson and the remaining staff made a break for it. They didn't tell Gunderson, because they knew Gunderson would tell me. And Johnson had decided early on that they were going to leave me behind because apparently, the middle of a war zone was the perfect place for Johnson to give me a final fuck you.

The Russians quickly recaptured everyone and paraded them back into camp the next day. They kept them in a holding cell made out of an old shipping container. When night fell, there was a lot of screaming and yelling, but no one would let us leave our tents to see what was happening.

By morning, the container was gone.

New prisoners came to the camp—all of them Russian defectors.

After a while, Gunderson and I had the lonely distinction of being the only Americans left.

It had to be past midnight now. It would be hours before we'd see the sun again, but at least it felt like the darkest part of the evening was behind us. Not for the first time, I was glad that we'd at least gotten to spend the dark days surrounding the winter solstice inside the prison camp.

I could see Blondie coming back off in the distance. He had found another bit of shrub to add to the fire. He looked surprised when he reached me. "I thought you would be asleep by now."

"Don't know if I can drop off."

"Why not?"

"I'm just thinking."

"What is there to think about?"

Well, *there* was a question I wasn't going to answer truthfully.

"What if we get stopped?" I asked.

"We won't."

"You seem certain of that."

"Every Russian fighter has been ordered to pull back," Blondie said, "None but stragglers are left in Alaska now."

"Stragglers like us?"

"Exactly. Rebels!" Blondie smiled as he jabbed his fist up. "The US likes rebels. I'm certain they'll like me too."

"Right."

"Why do you look so sad?" Blondie asked.

"It just feels like we're still in danger." I didn't even try to hide my fear. It was the truth, after all.

"Have no fear, my friend. Of course, this is a dangerous situation, but the worst is already over."

I could still feel the rock in my jacket pocket. The immovable stone was cutting into the thick fat of my thigh. "I wish I could feel that way, too."

Blondie walked up to me. The light of the half-dead fire turning his face a diabolical red. For a second his expression was blank, but then it relaxed into a smile. He dropped the bit of shrubbery onto the fire, and it roared back to life, bathing the camp in a yellow-gold light.

"Get some sleep," Blondie said. "You will feel better in the morning."

"I'm doing what I can over here, but it's not like I can cure insomnia with willpower."

I hadn't been sleeping more than an hour or two a night over the last few days. If something happened, I wanted to be ready. My babushka would be deeply disappointed if I died without a fight.

"My friend, I wish I could do something to put your mind at ease."

"The only thing that will ease my mind is a warm bed, a full meal, and the loving arms of the US armed forces."

"I agree! Even though I am a little concerned about how the last one will play out."

I tried to chuckle and mostly succeeded. "Look, don't let my insomnia keep you from resting. We have a big day tomorrow. We might reach the checkpoint."

"I would not feel right if I had to watch you suffer." Blondie's eyes had suddenly become hyper-focused. Trained on a target somewhere in the back of my skull. "Don't worry. If you have another sleepless night, you will not go through it alone. I will sleep as soon as you do."

He settled down close to me, and fear twisted my guts like a knife. I couldn't get away with faking sleep or sleeping lightly with him this close.

But if I actually went to sleep, I was certain I would never wake up.

I noticed his hair first.

There wasn't a lot of color in the yard. The coats were gray. The boots were black. The layers of ice under our feet were always being stamped into brown mush. But his hair, blond as a field of wheat in the sunshine, stood out.

I could see he wasn't like the other defectors. Even before he walked up to me, meeting my eyes and offering a sad, gentle smile.

"I'm sorry about your friend."

Gunderson had sworn he was just tired, even after the coughing fits sent him to the infirmary. He said he was going to make it. He had to. His family was waiting for him.

I knew his wife and daughter were dead. I'd heard the shots, but if believing they were alive kept him alive, I wasn't about to tell him otherwise. The last time I visited him, he told me things would be better soon—it was only a matter of time. In a way, he was right.

I watched them load a box with what was left of Bill into the back of a vegetable truck. I took a strange sort of comfort in the fact that the cardboard coffin was new and unstained.

"Kind of them to ship him back home," I said, with a barely repressed snarl.

"Russian hospitality." The venom in the blonde man's voice equaled my own. Yet while Blondie's American accent was well-practiced, he couldn't hide the slight drawl when he said 'hosp'.

"Are you so down on your own countrymen? *Comrade?*"

Blondie jerked back at that. "You think I'm Russian?"

"I know you are. You've got an accent."

For a second, there was a cold sort of anger behind his eyes. But Blondie took a deep breath, and it was suddenly gone. "That does it. I must return to Moscow and fire my English tutor immediately. Can you make the arrangements with the sergeant?"

I snorted in spite of myself. "I thought you'd have more reasons than that to get back home."

He smiled at me. "I'm not exactly feeling hospitable when it comes to Russian hospitality."

We watched until the vegetable truck pulled out of the camp and disappeared down the road. I tried to walk away, but Blondie followed me.

I turned and stared at him.

"You were going to the mess hall, yes?" Blondie asked.

"I was. Where were you going?" I asked.

"Coming with you."

"That's not necessary."

"You and your friend always had breakfast together. I cannot let you eat alone."

Maybe I should have known better. But I didn't. In that moment, I just needed to talk to someone. I was the only one left, now—completely alone in this horrible, pathetic place at last.

"Sure. Why not? Are you getting gruel or gruel today?"

I must've dozed off, because some time later, I woke to the distant sound of stone on metal.

A blade being sharpened.

I cracked my eyes open.

Blondie was a few dozen feet away from the campfire. He was moving a thin, rough stone against the metal of the hunting knife. Each time the knife was twisted, bits of light reflected off of the dying embers of the fire. His shoulders hunched with the force of each swipe as he sharpened the knife. Each pull was so hard it made the metal sing.

Sing. Sing.

I forced myself not to act. We were in the wilderness. We were fighting for our lives. There were a lot of reasons why Blondie would be sharpening our knife.

But why was he sharpening it so far from the warmth of the fire?

Sing. Sing.

With a shaking hand, I started looking for my rock.

I couldn't find it. It had been inside my sleeping bag, pinched between my knees, and now it was gone.

I couldn't twist or flip over. Blondie would definitely notice.

I could feel myself starting to panic. I had to stop it. This wasn't the time to lose my head.

Could I really kill a man over sharpening a knife early in the morning? Being a morning person was a crime against nature, but it didn't deserve a death sentence.

I carefully cracked my eyes again and watched Blondie. Not just what he was doing, but the expression on his face. I couldn't see every line and wrinkle on that face, not from this distance with my eyes half-closed. But I could see what was missing. The light in his eyes, the light that normally illuminated his entire face, was gone. It was not a face that could be distracted or joked with or reasoned with.

It was a decisive face.

He'd made his decision, and the knife came with the decision he had made.

Maybe I wasn't the korova. Maybe I was just a liability. Either way, staying wrapped up like a burrito felt like a bad thing.

I slowly worked my fingers down the front of my outer coat. I carefully opened one snap at a time. I paused after each one, unsure.

Did Blondie hear the soft popping noise that came each time a cap sprang free?

Not yet.

I carefully pulled the zipper down on the bag. I tilted the pull at such an angle that the sound would be as faint as possible.

The singing stopped.

I stopped.

For a moment, there was nothing outside of the distant sound of the wind.

What had given me away? Had he heard the zipper? Had I said something and didn't know it?

I could make him think it was nothing. People made sounds in their sleep all the time. Who's to say I wasn't doing the same?

Pinching the fabric to stay around me, I rolled over with a sigh. Turning my back to Blondie.

I felt the smooth, warm rock bump my skin and roll with me. It came to rest against my leg, just above my knee.

Could I grab it in time? Should I grab it now?

Blondie could walk up and, in a heartbeat, stick the knife in my back.

He could slit my throat. Stab me through my temple.

He could do a thousand horrible things to me, and I'd never see it coming.

I heard heavy footsteps coming towards me. Felt him looming over me.

I tried to relax my face, even as my hands had a tight grip on my coat and bedroll.

He was my friend. My *comrade*. Right?

There was an anemic chuckle. I heard Blondie mutter a single word. "Lokh."

Idiot. Naïve fool. Hayseed. Sucker. Loser.

I forced myself to stay still until the footsteps faded away, and the metal started singing again. Then I grabbed the rock.

Strong like an ox my ass.

"Ask me why I'm so happy today," Blondie said, as he sat down at the table next to me in the camp's mess hall.

He'd been smiling all day. He actually whistled when we got what passed for lunch.

"Are you happy?" I asked, like the little shit I was. "I hadn't noticed."

"It's my birthday, and I got a wonderful present."

He let the pause drag on, and I rolled my eyes. "OK, fine. I'll ask. What did you get for your birthday?"

"Just a piece of paper." He carefully slid a laminated sheet of his paper out of his sleeve, just far enough so I could tell it was a map. I looked up at him, my eyes wide with surprise. He slid the map back into its hiding spot.

"That's a better birthday present than I got last year. Mom just gave me a toaster."

Blondie grinned. "You know, the Americans are down near the coast. They've already established beachheads at White Mountain and Koyuk. They're going to be making the final push. So it's been decided that things must be tidied up. The camp will be liquidated tomorrow. None of the prisoners here will be spared."

I froze, spoon in midair. "But I'm an American citizen." I knew the statement was stupid the minute it left my mouth.

"The only one left. Look around you. Only Russian defectors and Russian deserters left. Gunderson is dead. The bodies they delivered to the American Consulate will need DNA testing and dental records, and it can take weeks to sort that information out. You'll likely be gone before your government knows you're missing. No one's going to hold off on liquidating the camp just because you *might* be around."

"Well, fuck. What am I supposed to do now?"

"You could escape..."

"And end up like Johnson?"

"I meant you could escape with me. I might have given one of the guards a reason to look away. We will need a wire cutter, but right now someone could get beyond the outer defenses without much effort. Two people can escape as easily as one, yes?"

Something like relief was rushing through my veins. "No shit? I can't believe you pulled that off."

"It was hard, but I managed it. And I would like you to come. I know we haven't known each other long, but I can't leave you here to die. Can you be ready at two in the morning?"

"What, and leave all this behind?" I joked. "Of course, I'll be ready!"

Blondie laughed. "I will come for you."

As he walked away, I felt better than I had in months.

But then I looked down at the meager plate of rations, a plate I was about to lick clean.

There was no food left to steal, and walking to safety would take days.

When Blondie returned to our campsite, he walked quietly. Expertly.

His heavy boots made no sound as they pressed into the snow.

The way he drew the long hunting knife in one fluid motion as he approached my bedroll was calm and practiced.

He knelt and rested a hand lightly on the back of my coat.

He gave my shoulder a consoling pat, then he struck.

It was one quick stab and a pull. The blade slid across the space between my hat and coat collar. If I'd still been wearing them, he would've slit my throat to the bone.

Blondie froze. He could tell something was wrong. Maybe it was the lack of blood. Maybe slicing a man's throat had a distinctive feel. But he was confused, and he leaned over the coat, trying to see why his blade had missed the mark.

This was my chance.

I jumped out of the shadows and smashed the rock into the back of his head. The sickening crack of bone echoed off the stone like angry thunder. Blondie fell forward, his hands tangling with the bedroll.

"Motherfucker," I screamed, adrenaline racing through me. "You fucking bastard!"

He rolled over and looked up at me, clumsily trying to stand. His eyes twitched with pain and shock even as his mouth formed the same petulant pout Misha wore every time I'd kicked his ass.

I brought the rock down on his forehead, struck at the side of his head, he threw up his arms, and I pounded his forearms, his wrists, he dropped the knife and I struck again. And again. And again.

"Stop!" Blondie bellowed, blood sluicing down his face. I flinched, and he dove for my knees, leading with his shoulder. I pivoted and body-slammed the side of his chest. He hit the ground on his back with a satisfying thud.

"How did you..." —he spat a few teeth out and clutched his head— "How did you know?"

"Ya ne tvoya marionetka," I spat. "Ya ne *korova*."

The expression on his shattered face turned from pain to shock to shame.

Then I brought the rock down a final time.

When my head finally cleared, light was breaking on the horizon.

I needed to see if I could combine our dwindling supplies in a single pack. With a little effort and the wind at my back, I could make it to the beachhead myself.

But not yet.

In the blooming light of the dawn, the hunting knife gleamed like fresh hope on the snow.

White Mountain was at least a day's walk away. Longer with all the equipment I would have to carry.

And I was so very hungry.

§

You shouldn't become best friends with someone you meet in an internment camp, but it was hard not to like Blondie. It was hard not to see myself missing him when he was gone.

Blondie had given me hope after Gunderson was taken. He had kept me going through weeks of hard labor and days of grueling travel. He'd kept me alive and freed me from the camps.

In the end, were his intentions unreasonable? He had just wanted to live. So did I.

I don't exactly miss him, but I find myself thinking of him at the strangest moments—like when I'm standing in my C-Suite office looking for a way to inspire my team.

I suppose it's not that surprising.

He's not gone—not really.

A piece of Blondie will be with me forever.

PARTING MEMORIES
By Marília Bonelli

VINES SLITHERED ACROSS THE heavy wooden doors, intertwining to bar Michael's exit. This faded white tower and everything in it was Selina's to command—except him. He was just the monster she'd invited in.

"Goodbye?" Selina's voice cracked. "That's all you'll leave me with?"

Michael quickened his pace toward the door. He couldn't afford to hesitate. If he didn't leave now, he might never.

"Please." The song, a mixture of her feelings and intentions that he alone could hear, became a mournful melody seeping into his mind. "I don't like it when I forget you."

"I'm sorry." Such useless words left a bitter taste on his tongue. There was no way to spare her pain.

The floor rumbled, and the doors fully disappeared behind an entwined barrier of green.

He stopped, his back tensing.

Would her magic be enough to stop him? Except for the brief

misunderstanding when she first stumbled upon him at the edge of her territory, they'd never truly fought. Like him, the strength of her power could not be judged by her frail human appearance.

Her song soared in a desperate crescendo. "I can keep bringing you memories. You won't starve. You won't kill anyone."

"You shouldn't venture out either." This tower was her haven, but she left it regularly to gather memories from strangers—food for the monster. "You are the one who is hunted by what's left of your kind. Nobody cares about me."

"I do."

"That's not what I meant."

"Don't leave." Don't leave *me*, the song pleaded.

He faltered, turning around to meet her eyes. When had he ever heard her beg?

The first words she ever said to him were a threat. But things had changed. Her song had shifted around him, including him in her world. The outcast had fallen in love with the monster. And the monster...

"Your brother's killers have been getting bolder. It hasn't been a month since you were ambushed while out harvesting memories for me." She'd collapsed at the foot of the tower, barely able to return. Cradling her unconscious form in his arms, begging her to wake—that was the first time he'd felt fear. No, not fear. As he'd wiped the blood from her cheeks, it was terror that came.

An echo of the poorly entombed despair from that day reached out from its shallow grave and squeezed his heart. "I should hunt for myself."

Hunt.

Wasn't he merely wandering around until he found an unsuspecting human?

Maybe, if he fed more often, he wouldn't go too far. He had no desire to add to the collection of lifeless gazes, devoid of all urgency or reason, that stared back at him from his own memories. Selina's method was by far the more merciful choice, copying rather than forever stealing away all the memories that made them who they are. In that sense, she was the perfect companion for him.

Selina's eyes, normally a shade lighter than the vines blocking his path, grew darker. "If I let you leave, will you come back?"

Did she really mean to fight him?

His lips parted to say he wouldn't, but he'd always be tempted. Even if she forgot him as soon as he left, she'd remember him the moment he returned. That tether would always linger, threatening to drag him back. And he was selfish enough to come looking for her—for that elusive smile she'd had just for him. He could barely see a shadow of that version of her in the person facing him.

"If you're hungry, you can feed now. We'll talk about this later."

Michael's face twisted. Hadn't he taken enough from her? Her brother's childish laugh and her mother's final embrace tasted bitter as they swirled in his mind. These precious memories he'd devoured when he lost control, but she didn't care.

If she hadn't been isolated in this tower for centuries, she wouldn't have taken a monster as company. If not the sole survivor from her side of a war that had destroyed most of the human world, if not for loneliness, would she tolerate a creature who'd steal away the only remnants of her family?

A monster had been living too long in this empty tower.

And if one day she truly did not return from hunting in his stead, then what would it matter that he was here?

He walked toward her, and her song softened. She took his offered hand readily, despite the slight burning sensation whenever they touched—the monster's hunger reaching forth. Her eyes, like the song, filled with hope. He pulled her into an embrace so he wouldn't have to watch it vanish.

Slowly, he followed the song into her thoughts, into her memories. It was easy to find the ones he wanted, prominent as they were in her mind. Her muscles twitched when she realized what he was doing, but she'd already been ensnared.

"Don't—" The discordant melody gave one final frenzied burst as she tried to push him out of her mind.

Hair as dark as night fanned over his arms, burying his fingertips. Her body went limp as he began pulling, stealing away everything she remembered of him. Every word exchanged, every glance, every touch…

When it was all gone, he lowered her unconscious form gently to the floor, a tender kiss on her forehead his only indulgence.

Later, she would wake, a thick haze concealing the torn threads of her memories.

She wouldn't know that, for a while, an outcast and a monster had shared a tower at the end of the world.

Michael wiped at the wetness in his eyes. Did monsters have hearts? Could their hearts even break?

A wave of his hand and the vines parted, the earlier command forgotten from their mistress's mind.

The monster stepped out of the tower and into the nightmare of his own making. This time, she would be free from him. Sadness gave way to regret before he'd even reached the bottom of the hill, but no amount of remorse could ever restore her memories.

Once gone, some things could never return. Not even monsters with a broken heart.

SO WHAT?
By Marília Bonelli

MUST SHE LOOK AT their eyes? Clara was weary of seeing fear—or worse, nothing at all.

Under the watchful gaze of the old woman on the stretcher to her left, she moved on to the next gurney. She stopped in front of the thick zippered bag, wringing her hands until she inadvertently snapped her gloves.

A burst of chaos descended upon the corridor as three people, all covered in white, rushed past her, navigating a small cart as if racing against an invisible opponent. Clara pressed herself against the wall. Distant shouts grew fainter as they moved onward until all that remained were the indistinct sounds of machinery somewhere nearby.

Clara drew in a deep breath to steady herself, and the stench of dead things that no amount of antiseptic could hide seeped into her lungs. Or maybe that was a figment of her imagination.

The hospital walls, a mixture of off-white and some undefined shade between green and blue, did nothing to help with the feeling of suffocation.

She took another, deeper breath through her mouth, and the mask plastered against her face, sucked in with everything else.

A flurry of footfalls rose and fell the next corridor over, feeling very distant.

Clara reached over and slowly dragged the zipper down, glancing self-consciously at the old woman still staring at her. She almost apologized for the added reminder of what might await these people. There was something cruel about placing the dead and the dying in a single file, a macabre assembly line headed toward the same final destination.

She wasn't much better though. She was, after all, forcing them to face what was inside each of those silent bags. Pulling back the plastic, Clara glanced briefly at the face. It was too round and the nose too big. She closed it up.

Resisting the urge to look back at the old woman, she turned the corner to the next corridor, where another queue of living and dead awaited.

She caught a glimpse of white as a nurse ran past her, and then she was left to her own devices once again. At first, Clara had felt like hiding every time she saw hospital personnel, sure she'd be thrown out for breaking the rules. She needn't have worried. The hospital staff was so overwhelmed that even the patients weren't guaranteed attention. It was unlikely they'd waste their time on a healthy-looking ambulatory specimen.

Clara continued with her quest until one bag blurred into the next. Unzip, pull back, zip up. Was she now part of the assembly line as well? Some deviant quality control perhaps.

The next bag was not like the rest. She blinked at it, then looked toward the next ones down the line. Her hand trembled. They'd run out of body bags. The next ones were giant-sized— well, human-sized to be precise—black garbage bags. Careful not to lose the tag that was tied onto one end, she undid the knot to look inside. It was a man no older than fifty. She wasn't sure whether to be happy or sad. As much as she wanted her quest to be over, she really didn't want to find her grandfather wrapped up like garbage, waiting to be taken away.

Clara moved on to each new bag, trying not to pay attention to anything but the task at hand. She turned another corner and started to move to the next bag when she froze. The image was different enough that it shocked her out of her daze—thankfully, before she'd reached out and touched the person.

A living person.

The man had a transparent bag over his head, which was connected to an oxygen cylinder. Clara hadn't thought anything else could surprise her, but this did the trick. What next? Were they going to run out of oxygen?

Hoping the man hadn't noticed she'd briefly mistaken him for the wrong end of the assembly line, she finished going through the bags on that corridor as well.

Nothing but a dead end awaited her when she was done. She took off the gloves, reversed them, and put them in her pocket. She'd likely need them later. This was the last pair she'd have until the pharmacies stocked up again.

She unlocked her phone automatically, a nervous habit. The picture of a smiling trio lit up the screen. She didn't want to look at that either. It was just as painful as looking at the people around her and even more wounding—a reminder of what she'd lost.

Coming to life in a flurry of buzzing and vibrating, the phone almost fell from her hand. Her brother's face smiled up at her from the screen.

"Clara?"

"Hi, Anderson. Any news?"

"The hospital called. They said they found Grandpa. They said you can go sign the papers."

The questions of where and how got stuck behind the lump in her throat, but she managed a hoarse goodbye before hanging up. Quick steps took her back past the living and the dead, but she didn't dare see if any had moved to the other end of the assembly line.

The reception area was just like the rest of the hospital—eerily empty of staff, and full of patients. After a brief conversation with the person on duty, she was directed to the young man who'd taken her to the morgue earlier that day when they couldn't find her grandfather. Gabriel, his name tag read. He gave her some paperwork to sign and handed her a bag of belongings.

Clara stopped before she'd even written the first letter of her name. Clumped together with a small pile of change, sitting on top of the crumpled image of a green hummingbird and half-hidden by the larger coins, was a small golden chain. Was this some kind of twisted game?

"This is a necklace…"

Gabriel stared back at her.

"These look like a woman's things." Clara looked at the body bag, already reaching for the gloves.

Gabriel was faster. He unzipped the bag and pulled it back. A woman, face wrinkled by time and graying roots showing beneath a blondish dye, lay inside. Clara handed him back the bag of someone else's possessions. She reached for her phone, stopping herself before she called her brother.

"Did we look through the extra refrigerated units?" Gabriel asked, his eyes scanning the tag.

Clara shook her head. They'd only looked through the bodies in the morgue; she'd looked through the rest of the bodies in the hospital herself.

He led her outside through a back door. "Wait here for a bit and we'll go check. I just need to report this."

By *this*, he meant the woman that had been labeled as her grandfather. Clara nodded wearily. Would that woman's family also be looking for her, checking body bags one by one like she had?

Clara drew in a deep breath, and warm air filled her lungs. She'd expected it to feel stifling, to match her frame of mind, but it didn't. It was a bright sunny day. That felt wrong somehow, but truly, the weather wouldn't care about their petty suffering. Even beautiful days such as this saw death and disaster; not every funeral brought forth rain clouds like in the movies.

From the shaded spot by the side of the building, she reached toward the sunlight. It warmed her skin, but inside she still felt cold.

Her grandpa always teased her that she loved the shade too much. *If you were any whiter, you'd be transparent*, he'd say.

On a day like today, he'd be sitting in his garden, watching the birds take turns grabbing food from the little feeder he'd set up. And then the dogs would bark and scare his feathered friends. Grandpa would be left to explain to the dogs—as if they were another set of grandchildren—that they shouldn't do that.

A smile slipped through. The dogs never changed, of course, but Grandpa always patiently explained in the same tone he used when telling her to eat more veggies. Or maybe it was the other way around, and he'd used the tone that was meant for the dogs for his misbehaving grandkids.

The sound of crying drew her attention to her left, further along the side of the building. A small group of hospital workers had established an impromptu rest area underneath the shade of a termite-infested tree. A young man was lying on the ground, one arm covering his eyes as he slept. Even unconscious, he did not seem at peace. A girl, maybe a couple of years younger than Clara, was crying her eyes out, hugging an older woman—in a mask and face shield—who comforted her.

"Hey!"

Clara turned to find a man standing next to a newly arrived van. "Do you work here?"

She shook her head, eyes going to the writing on the van's back door: Eternal Rest Funeral Home.

Gabriel came out at that moment, seeing the mortuary van. "What do you have?"

"I just need death certificates for these three so we can take them down to the cemetery."

Clara had heard that funeral homes were now taking the deceased directly from their homes to the cemetery. The hospitals were busy enough with the living—not to mention their own dead.

Gabriel turned to her. "I'll be right with you."

Clara nodded, averting her gaze when the van's doors opened. But she didn't want to watch the hospital workers either, so she tilted her face up to the clear blue skies and closed her eyes.

It was a while before Gabriel called her back over.

Clara pulled out her phone and showed him the photo of her and her brother with their grandfather. She'd already shown it to him, but she doubted he'd remember. "This is my grandpa."

The man nodded, looking at the screen. Out there in the harsh sunlight, she could see his eyes better.

Tired eyes... No, dead eyes—no more alive than those of the bodies he had to oversee.

How many days had it taken him to get that way? How many bodies? One hundred a week? Two hundred? More?

She wasn't even sure how many body bags it had taken her to stop looking at their eyes. If she saw as many as him over the course of only a few weeks, maybe her eyes would look like that as well.

Her gaze lowered to the picture on her phone, looking into her own smiling face.

She trailed behind Gabriel absentmindedly until they came to a stop next to a dirty white trailer-looking structure sitting in the small parking lot behind the building.

Gabriel walked her over to the door. As he opened it, a blast of cool air assaulted her, battling the warmth brought by the sun. Inside, body bags were lined up on shelves, pushed together for maximum occupancy.

As Gabriel checked the first couple of bags, Clara morbidly wondered if this refrigerated trailer-thing had originally been designed for food.

"Can I see the photo again?" Gabriel asked.

A brief flicker of hope came. She craned her neck to catch a glimpse of the body he was looking at. "That's not him."

He deflated. "Sorry, he's not here then."

It would do her no good to yell at him. She'd already screamed and raged all she could that morning. Nothing else would come out.

She stood there as he closed the trailer back up.

"Have you tried the cemetery?" he asked.

"No."

"He might have been sent over by mistake. It's a long shot, but…" He shrugged a shoulder. "And if he's still here, we'll find him."

Clara nodded, staring out at the jammed parking lot. A car door was open, someone's foot hanging out as they slept in the backseat. Probably waiting for news of some sort, too.

"Are you coming back inside?"

She shook her head, glancing toward him. "Thank you."

Clara rounded the building, following the thinning and thickening paths of shade along its side. A drop of water from an air conditioner fell onto her head as she stepped over the puddle it had left on the ground.

Back at the entrance, she called her brother again. "It wasn't him."

A long breath came through, then silence.

"I've already looked everywhere here."

"Clara…"

A cool breeze tossed her bangs into her face, further stinging eyes that were already red and swollen.

"My boss said I can get off work a couple of hours early. Where should I go?" Anderson asked.

Her eyes shut as she leaned against the outer wall. Was this something she was supposed to know?

It wasn't an unusual question. Nor was it an unusual assumption that she would give him an answer. As the eldest sibling by five years, it had mostly been up to her to take care of him. After their mother ran off with another man, Dad had dropped them off at their grandfather's house and never returned. But they'd never been alone. Grandpa had always been there, a steady force at their backs, holding them up. Even at twenty-four, she felt like a sapling whose support had suddenly collapsed.

"Clara? Are you still there?"

She nodded stupidly for a moment. "Yeah, still here."

"Are you going home?"

As a dentist's assistant, she wouldn't have a job to go to until the quarantine was lifted. But no, she couldn't go home. Not yet.

She straightened, brushing the hair from her face, and stopped as she was about to wipe her eyes. Reaching into her left pocket—not the one with the gloves—she pulled out the small tube of alcohol gel. She squeezed out a tiny drop and spread it along her hands. They had to make it last.

"No, I'm going to stop by the cemetery first."

"What? Why? They already sent Grandpa there?"

"I don't know." A bitter laugh made its way from her throat. She barely even recognized it. "Nobody knows."

"Do you want me to meet you there?"

"I don't know. I'll call you when I get there."

"Okay. I'll try to get off work as soon as possible."

Clara wasn't sure which she preferred. If he didn't leave work early, he could stay away from all this, from seeing so many dead faces that his insides would feel numb. She took a moment to gather her thoughts. She wasn't sure how to get to the cemetery and had to look it up online. It would take her a couple of buses to get there, but she probably shouldn't take an Uber.

She paused again and sent her brother a message, asking him to notify the Uber driver who took them to the hospital that their grandpa had tested positive. There had been little doubt at the time, but they'd promised to let him know just the same. It had been too late at night to beg any of their friends to drive them, and the reply from the emergency service might as well have been a busy signal—no ambulances were available.

As she crossed the small road that looped in front of the hospital entrance, she had to weave between the parked ambulances. That's where they'd all been hiding. Their back doors hung open, and they were all full—an outer supply chain for the assembly line inside.

Clara watched a man in his forties hold on to an oxygen mask inside one of the ambulances. He looked so scared.

Even her grandpa had looked scared when they brought him in… but then he smiled. Even though he was wheezing and having trouble breathing, he smiled at her—for her. She wished she could've done more than just stand there.

Tears fell from her eyes, and reality hit her in the face again. *Crap.* She couldn't even afford to cry. A wet mask was useless.

The first bus wasn't too crowded, and only one person was blatantly ignoring the local directive to wear masks inside public transportation. The lady was sitting with a friend a couple of seats behind Clara. Clara could hear her friend nagging her about putting on a mask.

"This is ridiculous. Everyone's being so paranoid. I've already had it, no big deal. Not being able to breathe well for a while was annoying, but it's not the end of the world."

Clara's eyes narrowed on the woman, wishing she could drag her in front of the captive audience at the hospital to make her arguments. To them, breathing was kind of important. Perhaps if she hadn't been running on fumes for most of the day, she would have argued back.

The woman noticed her glare and huffed, but because of either her friend's steady hand on her arm or the glares of other passengers, she said nothing more and finally put on her mask.

Clara's relief at exiting the bus was but a temporary condition. She got rid of one anti-masker only to be surrounded by dozens more. She hadn't seen them from the bus, but a large gathering of people—sixty or seventy at least, most of whom were maskless—blocked the other side of the highway. The ones who did have masks on were wearing them more as an accessory around their necks. Maybe they had gills.

The crowd swarmed along the asphalt, swooping down and banging their fists against the cars that dared to try passing. Some honked their horns in support, others tried to break through the disturbance by force, but the swarm continued unaffected.

Clara watched them go by, chanting and shouting in their rage, protesting against social distancing measures. Apparently, it was too cruel.

Wasn't death crueler?

Her own mind had gone around in circles all this time, thinking about the chain of infection that resulted in this particular horrible end for her family. Her grandpa had to have gotten it somewhere. But where?

Was it the person in line behind him at the store who lowered their mask to sneeze? Was it the delivery boy who gave him his change? Was it Uncle Fred who insisted the mask only needed to cover his mouth and not his nose? Or was it some stray little virus particle, floating in the wind?

Was it her brother, who couldn't afford to stop working?

Was it her, who'd stood in line for two hours at the pharmacy to buy the alcohol gel?

Did she even want to know?

The protest leaked onto her side of the highway, forcing cars to brake as protesters shouted into their megaphones, ranting against the injustices they perceived.

Perhaps they had no family, no grandparents to think of. They might have no friends, no acquaintances they'd rather not kill. Or maybe a person's life was not worth the price of these inconveniences.

They were like drunk drivers, complaining about zero-tolerance laws even though others died as a direct result of their actions. But why should they care? Like the drunk drivers, if they killed someone, it would rarely be themselves.

The sea of faces went by, mocking her under the protection of the golden-green colors of the national flag.

She couldn't remember when that beautiful flag had become so ugly, when it had become a shield everyone could hide behind.

Maybe this is how the world would end someday—with people protesting against an imaginary foe while the world collapses around them.

The bus she was waiting for waded through the crowd, honking its horn to get the protesters to move. Clara almost shouted out to them, inviting them to come along. Maybe they'd be more useful at the cemetery. Protesting against death itself would make more sense to her than this.

The second bus was less crowded. Not too many people needed to head out this way in the middle of the day. Exhausted, she closed her eyes and almost missed her stop.

She'd been to the cemetery once before when she was around five years old. Her grandma had been the one to leave them then. It was the only time she'd seen Grandpa cry.

The long road from the bus stop to the cemetery was much different on foot. It was cooler, for one, enshrouded by an endless row of eucalyptus trees. Twigs snapped beneath her old sneakers, but other than that, she heard nothing but the rustling of leaves. The smell reminded her of the home she'd grown up in before the eucalyptus trees had to be cut down due to disease.

A few cars passed her along the way, hopefully with less daunting quests than her own. Perhaps less daunting, but maybe no less painful.

As she stepped out of the road, she came to the path that led to the funeral home located on the premises. The parking lot was filled with cars. This would not be unusual, except that services were not currently permitted. Despite the dozens of cars, she saw only two people. Maybe the cemetery itself was swallowing them up.

The small funeral home was empty, its doors locked, but finally, she heard sounds of life—contradictory as it may be—from behind the building, where the graves were located.

As she rounded the corner, the world abruptly came to life as if she'd stepped through a portal. Mechanical monsters roamed the distance against a backdrop of more eucalyptus trees, surveying a sea of boxes.

No, not boxes.

Caskets.

Row upon row of caskets lined the reddish dirt, awaiting their turn. Several dozen people watched—some crying, others staring out at nothing.

Clara's hand shook as she reached for her phone. Where would she even start?

It hadn't even been two months since the worldwide pandemic had reached their borders—scary how quickly everything fell apart.

She walked toward the onlookers searching the crowd for an employee, but no one was wearing uniforms.

A girl held her mask in a hand as she cried quietly, another hand holding out her cell phone, livestreaming this travesty of a burial to her family.

"Well, we came straight here following the van."

Clara turned to see a man of about forty leaning toward a younger guy.

"Even the mortuaries don't have room anymore. The news said they'll run out of wooden coffins and urns by next week if the death toll stays the same."

Clara watched as the young man nodded, his eyes locked somewhere in the distance. She followed his empty gaze, wondering what else people could be buried in. Plastic containers, maybe? Or would they go into the ground as they were?

Even her beloved cat Lily had a proper burial, put to rest out back in a shoebox, along with pictures and a wreath of flowers. Grandpa had helped her arrange the cat like she'd been sleeping. She could only hope to see the peace of sleep when—if—she found him.

She looked around again for someone in a uniform. She couldn't very well start opening coffins. This wasn't a box of eggs at the supermarket.

The world fell deathly silent as the bulldozers stopped digging their trenches—was there a better name for it? Or did mass graves sound too much like the result of some out-of-control dictator's first attempt at genocide?

Picked up by the breeze, a woman's voice could clearly be heard wafting over from a nearby radio. *"Mr. President, we've now surpassed five thousand deaths."*

"So what? I'm sorry, but what do you expect me to do? That's life... Everybody dies at some point."

The distant rumble of a bulldozer started up again as it moved to the next location. Workers started lowering the coffins into the finished trenches one by one, side by side. Not too far away, the girl who'd been livestreaming started sobbing.

Clara clutched her phone harder. Her finger moved toward the back as it always did, unlocking it without a conscious purpose. The phone slipped from her hands, and her grandfather's smiling face stared up at her from the red dirt.

Everybody dies...

But did it have to be like this?

COMING HOME
By Autumn Shah

THE HOUSE LOOKED ALIEN to her after thirty-eight years away.

The sparse, yellowing grass and stunted palm trees seemed outlandish compared to the cold, inorganic habitat she had gotten used to. The yucca plants looked healthy and still grew out of the pebbled beds along the walkway.

A Christmas wreath hung on the door. The smell of the pine assailed her senses, so unused was she to little more than the acid-sharp smell of metal and the chlorine-tinged scent of regulated air.

Like her, the house did not look like it had aged almost four decades.

Christmas lights twinkled in sequence around the windows, and while they filled her chest with warmth, they also amused her, whisking her right back to the *Georgiana* and the blinking lights that communicated with the crew. Of course, the effect of the festive-colored bulbs was markedly different from the glaring, red warning of the Vital Systems Alert indicator or the multicolor blinking of the air pressure sensors.

She had tried to make the *Georgiana* a temporary home. She had taken a few mementos, cozy footie pajamas, and even some artwork done by her nieces. But she missed unexpected things like the feel of carpet beneath her feet, *weather*, and variations of color.

But it was Jiro she missed the most.

She never expected their separation to be so painful. They were used to long intervals apart. After all, the second year and a half of their relationship had been long distance. When they reunited, it was always as if no time at all had passed.

They had met at the University of Kyoto during her international fellowship program. He was marine biology, she was physics. Days in Kyoto parks, temples, and the university libraries. Nights sharing *kaiseki ryori*, and reading to each other on the pillow-laden futon in his apartment.

She lifted her arm to knock at the door, but she changed her mind and grabbed the door handle—another strange sensation, to open a door manually. Her legs weakened at the emotions roiling inside her, and she reached out for the wall. It wasn't only the return to normal gravity that made her unsteady on her feet.

She remembered their first kiss. She had thought it would never come. He was so shy, such a gentleman, not like the men she had dated back home in the U.S. They were at a sushi bar, nestled in a booth side by side. He reached for the wasabi. It may have been her who leaned in to make his reach a kiss. That first kiss, and the way he nuzzled her cheek afterward, sustained her through every absence thereafter.

The length of the deep space survey mission meant six years of cryosleep each way. She told him she would understand if he couldn't wait for her. But he had. She had watched him age through the video messages he sent for each week of her sleep. She relished those images and his one-sided conversations during the many years of the mission's blackout communication. When she woke up the second time, another six years later, his salt and pepper hair had made him look that much more distinguished, the crease above his left eyebrow had deepened to be that much more endearing. They remained who they were in each other's eyes.

He had stayed in this house waiting for her, despite the drying landscape around him, their friends moving to the ever-dwindling greener lands, and the places with more abundant water.

She walked the hallway, passing the antique Chinoiserie mirror, the Edo-period wall panel they had chosen together before leaving Japan. She paused at a framed photo of her and Jiro, taken just before she left. Their brindle mutt, Nova, sat between them. On the console table was a flowerless vase, some unopened mail, and a photo of Jiro and a new dog, Atlas. A dog she had never met. Further down the hall hung another photo; Atlas graying around the muzzle, Jiro with lines between his brows and crisscrossing the hands that cupped the dog's face.

She could see the flickering light of the fire from the den, hear its crackle and pop. She imagined she felt its warmth already kissing her skin.

She turned into the room, and there, sitting on the ratty

brocade loveseat, was an old man. There was no denying it. His skin was sallow and sagged, but his dimples were just the same, as was the crinkle above his left eyebrow. He stared back at her with the same sense of wonder she was sure she exhibited.

"Mallory?" Jiro whispered as she turned into the room.

"Yes. It's me."

And before he could rise, she raced, on still-unsteady legs, to throw herself beside him and into his open arms.

This house was a vessel, as sure as the *Georgiana* had been. It was in his arms that was *home*.

BELOW PILGRIM'S TIDE
By J. Powell Ogden

LEIK'S MOM LOVED PENGUINS, which was the reason he was stuck in this rapidly deteriorating shitshow.

"Almost everyone else is gone," Leik told her. "What are we supposed to do?" He listened, pacing as she talked. When she paused to take a breath, he pulled his phone away from his ear and looked at his college roommate, Ru. "They want us to Uber to Plymouth."

"Your uncle's?"

"Yep."

Ru chewed on his lower lip. "Did they ask him?"

"Yeah. Apparently, a global pandemic convinced him to reopen Pilgrim's Tide just for us."

Leik's phone squawked in his hand. He lifted it back to his ear to hear the tail end of his mom's apology. "—the best option, dear. I'm so sorry."

Leik brushed his fingertips over his forehead, envisioning the awkward reunion with his uncle. "He hasn't let us visit for years, and he has those—"

"They're gone, Leik. Okay? He said you're welcome to stay there."

In the background, Leik heard Ru's mom shouting, "We're so sorry, sweetie! They won't let us off the boat. Margo, tell them—"

"Who's got it?" Leik asked.

"A staff member. A steward, I think."

"And what if Uncle Sven's got it?"

"He has more reason to worry he'll catch it from you, but he's fine. He has no symptoms, and he said he will wear a mask. Two masks." Even Leik knew you could be contagious before showing symptoms. "And if you do, you know, catch it, you're young. Healthy. You'll be fine."

"Then why can't we just fly home to Vegas?"

"Enclosed space. People packed in like teeth on dentures." She made an exaggerated shiver sound. "They're talking about droplets."

Leik heard someone cough. A small wave of panic gripped his heart. "Was that Dad?"

"He caught a cold. It's freezing here. Call the Uber people. Charge it." Margo Lund was drawing out her "a's" and dropping her "r's" so "charge" became "chaaj." Her childhood Bostonian accent was breaking through, which told Leik she was more tired and worried than she was letting on.

"Fine," Leik said, throwing up his hand. "I'll call you when we get there." He hung up.

Ru, whose parents had accompanied Leik's mom and dad on

the trip, flapped his arms. "Why did they have to take their first cruise to the South Pole?"

"Penguins," Leik said.

"Fuck penguins," Ru said.

"At least we have a plan now."

Until that point, the two had been scrambling. Lassiter University was one of the few schools in Boston that had reopened after spring break. Everyone else had emptied out their dorms and told students to stay home. The 'Rona was everywhere. Now, in early April, Lassiter was following suit. They had been told to be out by the end of the day, which was easy for kids who could drive home or had parents to pick them up. Not for them. They were from Sin City, too young to rent a car, and their parents were on fucking rockhopper safari.

While Leik ordered an Uber, Ru texted his girlfriend and untacked his posters from the walls. The Declaration of Independence. The cast of Hamilton—signed. A peacenik Ben Franklin with a word bubble erupting from his mouth. "Tax the dick." Rufus Ming's ancestors may have emigrated from China in the early nineteenth century to help build the railroads, but he was obsessed with American colonial history.

"Pack up as much as you can," Ru said, rolling his posters together. "We may never get back in here."

Leik surveyed his stuff. He hadn't brought much. He hadn't even wanted to come to Lassiter, but he hadn't really wanted to go anywhere else either. So, he'd followed Ru, his best friend since grade school, who had chosen the only university in the United States to offer four "Bright History Scholar" dorm options. Greeks Rule. African Empires. Freedom Rings. Medieval Conquest. Ru, a die-hard history fanatic, had a white wig propped on a wig stand, and Leik was stuck in 1776 taking classes like Fuck Your Future 101.

As Leik stepped over dirty laundry, using empty pizza boxes like snowshoes, the door of their tiny dorm room banged open and Tyranny stormed in. She walked up to Ru, grabbed the front of his Liberty Bell tee shirt, and tugged him in for one of her I'm-in-charge kisses. She was taller than Ru, so it was more of a pulling up than a dragging forward. Ru didn't object. Tyranny, a Medieval Conquest dorm dweller, had been sleeping with Ru since the fall semester ended. She let Ru go, pushing him back dismissively.

Ru grinned.

Tyranny said, "I need my dice back."

"Oh. Right." He dug his hand in his grubby jeans pocket and held the seven hand-carved gaming dice out to her.

She snatched them off his palm. "Thanks. Call me at midnight. Do not be late." She blew him a kiss and headed for the door, turning back around at the last second. "Look, you can stay with me. Leik, too."

Ru looked at Leik, the gleam in his eyes declaring they had been saved.

Leik said, "Her mom's not going to want two possibly COVID-positive college kids showing up on her doorstep."

"And your hermit uncle would?"

"I could ask her," Tyranny said.

Leik's face warmed as he considered going against his mom, being the third wheel, or worse—traveling to his uncle's, alone. Ru knew Leik better than anyone. He sighed and walked toward Tyranny, waiting in the doorway. He took her hands in his and pulled her closer. "I'm going with Leik, T."

This time, she softened in his arms as he kissed her.

Then she pushed him away and walked out the door. Ru glanced over his shoulder.

"Thanks," Leik said.

By the time they were loaded into the tiny Yaris that arrived to pick them up, there were pillows, towels, and blankets piled high on the backseat between them, duffels in the trunk and a leaning tower of snacks stacked on the front passenger seat. The snacks had won out over the lamps and shower gear. They left those behind.

The swarthy driver, looking all progressive-pirate with his gold earring and bright fuchsia bandana tied over his mouth and nose, tossed two surgical masks over the backseat, and Ru and Leik slipped them on. The masks felt like too much, like they were trying too hard in a pandemic that didn't yet seem real. No one talked until they were south of Beantown and headed toward Plymouth.

"Is he any better?" Ru finally asked. His voice was muffled under the blue and white, gauzy paper. "I mean, it's been years, right? Since the car accident?"

Leik looked up from his phone and out the window at the wind- and salt-battered buildings speeding by. It was really his fault Ru loved colonial history. Ru had joined the Lund family every summer on trips to visit his mom's brother and wife at their bed-and-breakfast, Pilgrim's Tide. the old house, which the two had lived in year-round, was south of Plimoth Plantation and clung to the edge of an eroding white cliff overlooking the ocean. Ru and Leik had flown kites there, swum in the ocean and traveled with his parents up to Boston, Lexington and Concord to sightsee. Uncle Sven had told the best stories around nightly beach campfires while his aunt baked authentic Norwegian Kringles for breakfast in the morning.

That all changed five years ago when Aunt Mills died.

"Sven never called it an accident," Leik said, eyes still on the window. "Sven called it roadside homicide." Leik had never wanted to talk about the details and Ru had never asked, but Ru was his best friend, and he deserved to know what he was walking into. "He and Mills were driving through South Carolina on their way to the Keys and stopped for ice cream. You know Mills loved her ice cream." Ru nodded, no doubt remembering the elaborate sundae bars she had set out for them and their paying guests on hot summer nights. "Mills' cone was dripping. She was distracted. She tripped and fell off a curb into the drive-thru lane, and a man named Lokkhart Loughlin plowed his shitty minivan into her. Her head got crushed between the bumper and the side of the Dairy King, and her eyes…" Leik couldn't bring himself to say what happened next, so he pointed at his eye and puffed his lips to make a half-hearted explosion sound that fizzled near the end.

The sides of Ru's mouth dropped down in disgust. "So, like,

her eyeballs were…"

"On the Dairy King's brick wall."

The man driving the car shifted uncomfortably in his seat.

There was more—weird as shit behavior from Uncle Sven—that had disturbed his whole family, but it could wait. Leik didn't want to talk about it all masked up, voices muffled, in a tiny Yaris with the driver listening.

"Ugh. Poor Uncle Sven," said Ru.

"Yep."

The sun had dipped below the craggy trees on the west side of the road by the time they turned onto the Pilgrim's Tide private drive. Thick woods closed in. The little car shimmied and shook as it skidded over loose gravel. Low-hanging branches scraped at the roof, and Leik was pretty sure Sven hadn't touched a mower or tree trimmer since the day Mills died.

The woods retreated, and the house loomed in the deepening twilight like a spiteful shock of dark, negative space. None of the lights were on, inside or out.

The driver craned his neck to look through the windshield. "You kids sure this is the right place?"

Leik clutched his seat, the word "no" flashing through his mind. There were motels in Plymouth, cheap ones empty of the summer hordes, and an even cheaper fishing lodge farther down the road. The lodge smelled like fish guts, and they'd have to share a communal bathroom, but anything was better than staying here in this lonely house with the uncle he hadn't seen in years.

"He's home." Ru pointed to the chimney. There was smoke. The driver left them on the chilly driveway with their belongings piled around their feet. He waved and wished them luck as he drove away.

Pilgrim's Tide was a two-story, faded clapboard, cedar shake-roofed, historic landmark. The last time Leik had seen it, which was before his aunt died, it had practically gleamed. Now, cobwebs strangled the outdoor light fixtures and fine, sandy grit caked the screens. An upstairs window was cracked. Not even duct-taped. At the back of the house, there were balconies, empty, peeking over trees at the ocean. In the quiet night, Leik heard waves crash against the rocky shore and his best friend's shallow breathing.

A snip of curling tape secured a handwritten note to the heavy oak door. Ru plucked it off, eyes squinting to read while Leik's zeroed in on what had been hidden behind it—a deep, coarse carving in the wood. Leik dragged out his phone, switched it to flashlight mode and shone it on the door.

"Shine that thing on the paper," Ru said.

"Look at this."

Ru looked up from the note. "Shit, is that…is that a Thor hammer?" Thick wood splinters dangled from the carving, jagged and mean.

"That wasn't here before."

"Sven *is* Norwegian," Ru said. "Tyranny's got a teeny one

tattooed on the side of her index finger. She told me Thor hammers bring good luck."

Leik bristled. "I know that." And he did. Those were the stories his uncle loved to tell. Viking legends. Bright, violent mythological bits of his family heritage. Greeks didn't rule. Vikings ruled.

Ru wrapped his hand around Leik's phone and directed the beam down at the note.

"Bastard," Ru said, smacking the paper.

"What?"

"He says the inside of the house isn't 'suitable.' He's having it painted for the reopening of the bed-and-breakfast this summer. He says we have to sleep in the carriage house down on the beach. How long are we supposed to stay there? It's only got a port-o-john."

Leik could hear his uncle's quiet, logical voice in his head. The note sounded reasonable but somehow off at the same time.

Ru scraped some of the grit off one of the tall, narrow windows next to the door and peered in. He pressed his forehead into the grime, splaying his fingers on the glass. "What the hell is that?"

Leik's stomach dropped. His mom said Sven had gotten rid of them. She promised. Ru stepped back and pointed through the glass.

Leik squinted through the spot Ru had cleared. Moonlight streamed in through the rear windows of the house, dimly illuminating the interior. All the furniture was draped with white sheets, but that was expected if it was being painted. What wasn't was the huge glass aquarium in the dining room to the left of the foyer. Seven feet tall. Five feet wide. Drippy mold grew on the inside of the glass, and a large tree trunk with spidery branches lay diagonally inside it. What Ru didn't know, didn't *see*, was there might be more tanks, just as big, spread throughout the house. This one was empty. He hoped they *all* were empty.

Leik's white-blonde hair lifted on a bleak ocean wind. The night was getting colder.

"A terrarium," Leik said.

"That's freaky, man. What was in it?"

Leik looked away and then back. The masks were off. The driver was long gone. The "more" about his uncle needed to be told.

"Snakes," Leik said.

"Your uncle had snakes?"

Leik could tell it didn't compute for Ru, that the former bright and breezy, full of laughter house had devolved into a derelict shell full of snakes.

"They're gone now."

"What kind of snakes? That's a damn big cage."

"After Mills died, my parents visited once against Sven's wishes. They took pictures. They wouldn't show them to me, but I found them on our shared drive. He had snakes. Venomous snakes. Taipans, Cobras, Boomslangs. More than a few. And on the dining room table, there were jars and tools, like small, medical-grade instruments. He refused to get rid of the snakes, so my mom said she called the city. It's against the local ordinance to own venomous snakes inside city limits, and they made him get rid of them. She said one of the local boys shot each one in the head, so like I said, they're *gone*."

"What were the tools for?"

Leik looked off to the side again, suddenly feeling very tired. It had been a shit long day.

"Leik?"

He slid his eyes back. "He was milking them. He said it was for—"

Ru's hand flew up. "No. I don't want to know." Then he crumpled up Sven's note and shoved it into Leik's hand. "Brilliant plan. Remind me to thank your mom." He trudged back to their stuff. "Let's go. The carriage house will be just fine."

Calling the structure huddled against the base of the cliff a carriage house was generous. First, it was accessed by seven flights of rickety stairs bolted precariously to the side of the cliff behind the main house. Second, it was more of a shed. It had no power, no heat, and no indoor plumbing. Sven had, however, tried to make it welcoming.

The concrete floor had been swept, and the two windows were free of cobwebs. Two blown up air mattresses, each with a sleeping bag, sheet, and soft pillow wrapped in a clean white pillowcase, lay on the floor. Aunt Mills had always taken pride in the luxurious, crisp white linens she provided her guests. On a small wooden table, boxed in by two ladderback chairs, there was a pitcher of iced lemon water, a lantern and a bowl of apples. Although the apples were a sweet, bed-and-breakfasty touch, he was glad they had brought the snacks—chips, string cheese, Oreos, and a half-full box of protein bars.

Down by the ocean, the chill wrapped around Leik's shoulders and settled in. After they organized their things and ate, Leik claimed an air mattress, crawled into a sleeping bag, and rolled onto his back. He shone his phone's flashlight up at the ceiling, restless.

"Better turn that off," Ru said. "Battery life."

"My parents should have come back, invited or not," Leik said. "*I* should've—"

"He didn't want you here."

"My uncle's got no kids. Pop and Grams are dead. He just has us."

"Did your parents want to come?"

Leik sighed. "My parents don't push themselves on people. It's not their thing."

"They push themselves on you."

"No, they don't."

Ru propped himself up on one elbow, making the rubbery air mattress wheeze. "Dude, you came to Lassiter because of them."

Leik circled the light lazily over the ceiling, irritated. "I came to Lassiter because of you."

"No. You came to *Lassiter* because your parents decided you had to enroll in a four-year college after high school. You wanted to take a gap year in Scandinavia."

Ru's statement smacked of insult, and Leik dished it right back. "So? They're smart. I listen to them. What are you going to do with a stupid history degree?"

Ru was quiet. Leik felt bad for saying what he'd said, but not bad enough to take it back. The whir of insects and endless, curling surf sound-bombed the silence, and Ru rolled onto his side away from Leik. "Whatever it is," he said, "it's my life. I'll be the one calling the shots."

The ear-shattering chorus of Green Day's "American Idiot" catapulted Leik from deep sleep. He fought his sleeping bag, unsure where he was, and Ru threw his hand out to steady him. "It's my alarm." He yawned, unzipped his bag, and rolled awkwardly off his air mattress. "I have to call Tyranny."

"Are you serious, man?"

"I love her, dude."

"Oh my God."

Ru held up his phone. He stood up and walked around their spare oasis. "I got no bars." He walked out onto the beach, tripping over the threshold. "Fuck. You got any bars?"

Leik dug his phone out from under the air mattress. There was a half-eaten Oreo stuck to the face. He flicked it off. "Mine's dead."

Ru held his phone high above his head and walked toward the cliff stairs. "Maybe we can get a signal up top."

Leik flopped back on his mattress. The temperature had dropped to the point his breath was fogging in front of him. The last thing he wanted to do was climb those swaying steps in the cold, at midnight, only to have it shoved in his face again that his uncle was…he didn't know what.

Ru's voice reached through the dark. "Aww, c'mon. We've seen spiders and bats on those steps. There might be…" He made a fake choking sound. "…poisonous…snakes."

"There are no snakes!" Leik shouted back, but he stood up, stretched his back, and dragged his sweatshirt on. He stuffed his feet into his shoes and grabbed Ru's. As always in their long, rambling friendship, their argument had already faded into the past, gone but not totally forgotten. It still irked Leik that Ru had trashed his lack of a solid plan, his caving to his mom's insistence on launching into a four-year degree right after high school. Or maybe that was wrong. Maybe he was pissed at himself.

Leik lobbed Ru's shoes at him, waited for him to slip them on, and the two began to climb. To the east, the full moon rose high above them, silvering their backs and casting their shadows onto the rocky cliff. Halfway up, Ru, slightly pudgy around the middle, was breathing hard. "Fuck. I still got no bars."

The old wooden stairs swayed under their weight, and Leik held the railing tight, worried a tread might give way, and he'd plunge through. Close to the top, he suddenly stopped. Ru bounced into him from behind. The splintery railing had vibrated. The stairs, too. It was a low, chest jiggling rumble that came up through the soles of his shoes and buzzed in his fingertips. The vibrations swelled for several long seconds and then dissipated like a massive train going by. "You feel that?"

"Felt like an earthquake," Ru said. And he brushed past Leik, sprinting up the final flight with Leik at his heels. At the top of the cliff, on the back lawn of the bed-and-breakfast, Ru leaned over, hands braced on kneecaps, catching his breath. Leik, only slightly more athletic, looked over his shoulder at the ocean through the dark, shifting trees. Despite the cold, sweat trickled down his back. "Do they have earthquakes in New—"

He was startled to silence by the creak of the back door opening. His nerves already jangling, he pulled Ru back into the shadow of the trees. A northeast wind gusted, rustling the leaves and bowing branches.

"*What?*" Ru said.

Leik slapped a hand over Ru's mouth and pointed at a man walking across the damp grass toward the well in the center of the backyard only twenty yards from them. The man was haggard, had a wiry, unkempt beard reaching halfway down his chest and wore a heavy, moth-eaten, cable-knit sweater. He carried a wide metal bowl with both hands.

"Dude, that's Sven," Ru whispered.

Leik's heart lurched. Something was seriously wrong with his uncle. He opened his mouth to call out to him. Then the screams began—startling, wordless screams of anguish or pain—and with them, the ground started to shake again. It was a more subtle quake, and if he hadn't felt the tremor on the stairs, Leik would have thought he was imagining it. The tremor swelled with the screams and subsiding with them, too, into the quiet night.

His uncle paid the shrieking no mind, which made the hair on the back of Leik's neck stand up. Sven strode to the well, dumped some liquid down into its dark, watery depths and returned to the house, disappearing inside. With moonlight splashed against the back of the house, Leik could see the back door clearly as it slammed shut. Carved into the wood was another Thor hammer—this one at least three feet tall.

Ru's phone chimed with a call coming in, and Leik nearly popped out of his skin. Ru slapped the phone to his ear. "Not now, Tyranny." He hung up on her.

The horrible screaming echoed in Leik's mind. "Let's call the cops."

"And tell them what? We heard a dude screaming? They'll probably wonder who we are sneaking around this house. You think your uncle will come to the door and tell them when they knock? You *saw* him."

Leik ran nervous fingers through his hair.

Ru pulled up his phone and started madly typing.

"What are you doing?"

"I'm telling T to call the FBI or some shit if I don't text her back in a half hour." He shoved the phone in his back pocket. "We're going in."

Leik looked at him, incredulous. "And do what?"

But Ru was already hunched over and lumbering toward the house like a SWAT team of one. Leik felt the weight of his dead cell in his back pocket. He wanted to call his mom. Tell her what was going on. Ask what he should do. Sven was her brother after all, and it was *her* fault he was here—not just here at Sven's, but a refugee from Lassiter University. Ru was right. If Leik had done what he wanted, he would be in Norway right now, working in some little mom-and-pop café, running down his family history, and exploring the fjords and glaciers on weekends. Maybe with some pretty Scandinavian girl thinking he was cute and keeping him company. Instead, he was trapped in some freaky horror show with a balled-up, have-to-do-something-feeling slicing through his chest. From the back of the yard, he watched Ru cup his hands around his eyes and peer in a side window. If the crazy-ass uncle he'd seen carrying that bowl found him trying to break in…

"Damn it, Ru." Leik jogged across the yard and dragged Ru back from the dirty glass. "The screams were probably just the TV. Maybe Sven's put in one of those kick-ass home movie theaters, you know, for the summer guests."

"You literally just said to call the cops."

"Look, I don't want to piss him off. And—"

"You heard that scream. You know what it sounded like."

Torture. It sounded like torture. But this was his uncle. His frail, seventy-year-old uncle who used to read them stories and make frothy root beer floats and plant flags in painted flower pots on Independence Day.

"Ru, this is…" Leik was going to say stupid, but he stopped short because Ru was looking up at him, wide-eyed and earnest. Ru believed in heroes. Paul Revere and his lantern. Hamilton and his pen. For a moment, the shadows clinging to his friend morphed, and Leik saw him in a dusty wig and tri-pointed hat with a pitchfork clutched in his fist, ready to prod Leik into action. Ru was the hero of his own Freedom Rings story, and that story had begun when he heard those goddamned screams. Leik squeezed Ru's arm. "There was more than one snake cage, Ru. Okay? My uncle's batshit. We don't know what we'll find in there."

"That's kind of the point." Ru shook Leik's hand off. "Help me get this screen off."

Leik sighed. He had climbed in and out of his share of windows, and he flexed the screen expertly with his fingertips, digging the tip of his pinky into the small crack, and popped it off. Ru slowly pushed up the window. Behind them, an owl hooted from a nearby tree, and Leik's heart surged against his ribs. Ru grabbed the windowsill and hefted himself up and over. Leik dropped softly onto the bare wood floor of the dining room. Around him, the sheet-draped dining table and chairs looked like sunken sailboats, listing at the bottom of a murky sea. The snake habitat near the far wall was a monstrous science project gone awry.

Leik held his breath and listened for footsteps, a squeaking floorboard, faint exhalation, hissing—more screams. Nothing. The silence was worse. At least screams could be located, run toward or away from. If you heard screams, you still had a choice.

Ru tiptoed to the kitchen doorway and peeked in. From his place by the window, Leik saw dozens of empty, prepper-sized water jugs cluttering the kitchen table and stacked against the wall. Ru backtracked, and Leik followed him into the living room.

"Damn. You weren't kidding," Ru whispered. He shone his phone's light around.

More moldy serpentariums pushed up like stalagmites, glinting among the sheet-covered couches, chairs, and coffee tables. They were empty. Given what they'd heard, that gave Leik little comfort. Above a blackened hearth, dozens of Mills' sundae cups were crowded together, used over and over as candle jars until they were coated with misshapen globs of wax. Sven must have burned through every one of her little candles before succumbing to the dark.

Behind him, Ru whispered, "There's no paint, Leik." Leik turned around as Ru swept his phone's flashlight over the floor. "No paint cans, no rollers, no scrapers or drop cloths." Ru walked through an archway into the back hall, a hand on his hip.

A swell of grim uneasiness rose in Leik's gut.

The stairwell at the rear of the house held two sets of stairs. One flight led to the upper guest rooms, the other down to the cellar. To Leik's left, the back door's heavy brass doorknob was within reach. He almost grabbed Ru and dragged him toward it. With a twist of his wrist, they could be out of the house, gulping chilly night air, Thor's hammer behind them.

"Up or down?" Ru whispered.

Leik's palms began to sweat.

The floor creaked behind them. "Out."

Heat rushed through Leik's body, but he recognized the voice. As he turned, he moved to shield Ru. Back in the corner of the wide hall, in the suffocating shadows, his uncle rocked forward on Pop's old leather rocker, hands on his knees, something long and thin across his lap. He tilted his face up. "Leik, you need to go. Now."

From behind him, the light from Ru's phone crossed Sven in

jerky, found-footage fashion. In the shocking light, his uncle's eyes were sunken in a doughy face. His uncle's hair was tied back in a stringy man bun. Dry skin hung from his lips and small sores speckled his skin like he was deficient in some vitamin or mineral or hadn't seen the sun in years. If not for his uncle's pale, piercing eyes, Leik would have thought him a squatter. Homeless.

Sven Dahl stood up, moving quickly and not at all hampered by what appeared to be ill-health. He walked toward them, rubbing his index finger over the sharp tip of the slender rod in his hand. "Leik, these are scary times, but family helps family." His voice was rough, hesitant, like he hadn't used it in a while. "I left blankets and pillows for you down in the carriage house, and I'll have breakfast on the back deck in the morning. I'll order any supplies you need until your mom and dad can pick you up, but if you don't leave now, right now, the world is going to get a hell of a lot scarier."

"What's scarier than a global pandemic?" The question came out high and screechy, and Leik really, desperately, wanted to know, because his uncle's appearance hinted at some next-level, apocalyptic shit.

His uncle leaned forward, the smell of unbrushed teeth fanning Leik's face. "I need you to leave, boy. *Now.*"

Leik arched back, forcing Ru down onto the first step of the cellar stairs, and dropped his eyes to the object in his uncle's hands. It was an arrow. A strange, intricately carved arrow. Then, from the stairwell, down below, a voice warbled weakly.

"Help! Somebody?"

Leik looked his uncle in the eye. Below them was a warren of tiny rooms, half of which were only partially excavated and oftentimes rank with standing water. The voice rippled up the stairs again, sending shivers down his spine. "Is somebody up there?"

Leik's mind reached for a logical explanation. Anything was better than what his imagination was conjuring. "Who's down there?"

In front of him, his uncle's face contorted with despair, rage, and flat-out insanity. "He. Killed. Mills!" He gestured with his hands. The arrowhead jerked wildly toward Leik's throat. Leik grabbed the shaft and swung his fist, hitting Sven hard, square on the jaw. His uncle's craggy face arced left, his body tumbled forward. Then all three of them fell like lazy dominoes down the stairs.

"Get…off…"

Leik's ears rang with a high, tinny vibrato. He lifted his head. A trio of kerosene lanterns, lined up on the floor in the corner, stained the moisture-streaked, stone cellar walls a dim, oily yellow. Crushed beneath him, Ru pleaded again. "Get…off…"

Leik's palms throbbed. He tried to push himself off his friend, but a warm, heavy weight pinned him down. He reached behind him and felt his uncle's bony shoulder. His hand came away slick with blood.

"Leik…" Ru groaned.

Leik reached behind him again, grabbed his uncle's shoulder, and rolled sideways. A sharp pain lit up his lower ribs. Sven flopped onto his back, and Leik pushed up onto his heels, clutching his side and gulping air to keep from passing out. The arrow protruded from a deep red pool in his uncle's stomach. Panic sunk sharp teeth into Leik's gut. His uncle wasn't moving. He had to be dead. Heart pounding, Leik rubbed his face, smearing blood over his eyes, and glanced over his shoulder at Ru, wincing as his ribs lit up again. One of them had to be broken. "Are you okay?"

Ru sat up on the floor. "What the fuck just happened? What the—"

Sven's chest heaved.

Leik stood and skittered backward as the old man gasped. Sven's eyes stretched wide open. He reached for the arrow, touching its bloody fletching almost lovingly with shaky fingers. Then he looked up at Leik. "I found...I found this in his garden shed."

Leik's hands twitched at his sides. He couldn't fit his uncle's words into the current picture. He needed to get help. "Where's your phone, Ru?"

Sven's fingers fluttered around the arrow's shaft like he was considering pulling it out. He kept talking, his tone conversational. Almost rational. "I haven't fed him in four years. He's still the same." More words that didn't fit. Leik clutched his chest and pressed his back against the wall. Blood bubbled at the corner of his uncle's mouth.

"Ru! Your phone!"

Ru patted his pockets down, frantically searching. "I don't

know. I can't find it."

Sven sucked in his breath as he propped himself up on his elbows and dragged himself backward until he was leaning against the opposite wall. Blood spilled from the puddle in his belly, and Leik wondered if the arrow had gone all the way through. From down the dark hall, a tremulous voice with an Irish accent called out, "Please. *Please*, oh sweet Jesus Lord…I'm here."

Trembling, Leik gaped at his uncle.

His uncle looked resolutely back. "You don't know what we're dealing with here, Leik. He's dangerous."

Ru stood and limped to the corner. He grabbed a kerosene lantern. "I'm going to see who's back there," he said. "Are you coming?"

Standing between his bleeding uncle and his hero-wannabe friend, Leik flexed his shoulders, cooling blood slick across his spine. He forced his panic down. "I'll watch Sven."

Ru paused for a long beat, the lantern held out in front of him. Then he turned and limped down the hall.

"Who is it, Uncle Sven?"

"He's not human."

A shudder unsettled Leik's bones. He didn't reply. His uncle had clearly lost it. Absolutely, definitely lost it. The light of Ru's lantern rocked back and forth in the hall.

"Oh, fuck, Leik! Oh, fuck…"

Cold piled on Leik's soul like an arctic ice shelf collapsing. Keeping an eye on Sven and gripping his side, Leik grabbed a lantern and backed down the hall. The sound of heavy, labored breathing grew.

"In here."

Ru stood in the splintery doorframe of the last room. With great trepidation, Leik pushed his lantern into the darkness, and whatever nightmare scenario he might have envisioned, this—*this*—was far worse.

The greasy light of the lamp pitched and rolled on the exposed beams and earthen walls before stabilizing. Back in the corner, in front of a dank crawl space, a man was shackled to a huge rock. He wore soiled jeans and a torn undershirt. His face was gaunt, his limbs were skeletal and his forehead was pitted with scars. An ominous metal bowl hung above him on thin, rusting chains— the same bowl his uncle had emptied down the well.

The man just stared at them for a few seconds, hollow-eyed, mouth hanging slack. Leik blinked hard and long, trying to convince himself he was trapped in a nightmare. That he was still asleep in his narrow dorm bed up in Boston, safe. But the smell of rot, human filth, and mold wafted in and out of his nostrils.

"Let me go," the man said.

Back down the hall, his uncle gave a wheezy laugh. "He looks half dead, doesn't he? Don't trust what you see. He shapeshifts."

Ru stood very still in the doorway, petrified, his left cheek twitching.

Leik said, "Who are you?"

There was a long pause. Then the man said, "I'm from New Calhoun, South Carolina. I was kidnapped. My name is…" He swallowed hard. "My name is Lokkhart Loughlin."

Leik blinked again, a quick, mind-clearing shutter of his eyes. His mouth formed the words before he could temper them. "You killed Mills."

"You're her nephew."

"Yeah."

"Leik Riley Lund."

"Yeah."

"Let me go, Leik."

His uncle coughed. "Don't…don't listen to him, Leik."

Leik moved into the room, holding his lantern high, keeping his distance from the bound man whose hollowed eyes followed him. Looking back into them, it hit Leik like a stray bullet. The man knew his name.

The man's mouth quirked. "You can't possibly believe that… that…babbling, torture-porn-addicted, cesspool of a human skin bag down the hall."

No, Leik didn't believe his uncle, but the drive within him to fall in line with familial authority was strong. "What is it I'm supposed to believe or not believe?" Beside the man, a step stool leaned against the wall. Across from him stood a banquet table with a thick scattering of papers, photos and old books. He shuffled sideways toward it in the gloom.

The man looked up at the ceiling. His smartass façade crumbled. "For God's sake, let me go! I've been here for…I don't know how long. He drugs me. I'm starving. My wife must be out of her mind. My kids—"

"Look at the papers on the table," Ru urged.

"It's all there," Sven shouted. "Everything! Look at the picture of his house. The *tree*. You'll understand when you see it. You know the stories. If he hadn't killed Millie, we never would have known. His pride would have destroyed the world."

"Pride?" Lokkhart licked his dry, blistered lips with a dry, crusty tongue. "I live in a trailer park. I have junk cars in my front yard. My favorite restaurant is the Golden Corral, but only on Thursdays when it's two for one and drinks are free."

Ru said again, "Leik, the table—"

Leik shot him a look that shut him up. Ru could look at the papers. Ru could do something. But Ru was too terrified to set foot in the foul room. Leik knew he should back out, too, slowly, and search for Ru's phone, his uncle's, call for an ambulance, but the shackled man was mesmerizing. Heart hammering, Leik set the lantern down on the table.

On the far-left side, Aunt Mills' face smiled up at him from a pile of newspaper clippings about the accident, which had made national news because of the grisly way she died. Lokkhart's face was more subdued in his mugshot. Gaunt even then. Unrepentant. Leik knew the details, but he skimmed the articles anyway, feeling the loss of her all over again.

Lokkhart had slammed into his aunt, driving his wife's minivan with his two young boys, Nial and Vaughn, in the backseat. He was arrested and charged with vehicular homicide. There were no skid marks. Witnesses said the minivan sped up instead of slowing down, but his aunt had stepped into his path without warning. Lokkhart was acquitted and Uncle Sven, on the courthouse steps after the trial, had railed against the system that failed him.

Leik pressed his fist into the table. "You didn't even try to slow down."

"I never drive that tin can. The little monsters were fighting. I hit the gas instead of the brake."

"You don't sound sorry."

"Should I be? At least her death was quick. Your uncle has tortured me for years."

I haven't fed him in four years.

He's not human.

Leik shifted his eyes to the photos strewn across the center of the table. There were pictures of the dented van with its rear bumper wired on. Pictures of his family. His rotund, sunburned wife sitting beside a baby pool in front of a sagging trailer with two little boys splashing in the water. His wife raking leaves. His kids jumping in leaf piles. Making snowmen. Their trailer was on the edge of a deep green swamp, and beside it was a tree at least fifty feet tall. Leik lifted the photo, leaving bloody fingerprints on the border. The tree, his uncle said. Look at the tree. The tree was tall and twisted, maybe a Cottonwood, with squirrels' nests wrapped around branches near the top. Unremarkable. Leik dropped the photo on the table, creeped out by his uncle's voyeurism.

"See? He stalked my family." Lokkhart rattled his heavy chains. "He's sick. He needs help. I swear I won't say anything. I won't. I just want to go home."

"Home?" Down the hall, Sven laughed a wheezy, gurgly laugh.

"He was hiding from Thor. He chose the last place on earth the gods would look for him. Away from the sea in a stagnant swamp with a fat, homely wife and two white trash children."

Leik lost it. "What the hell is wrong with you? Thor? Really? Who do you think this guy is?" But even as he asked, his mind dredged the depths of his memory. He knew this story, didn't he? His eyes slid to the right, scanning the books on the table. They were old, stained, some missing pages. With trembling fingers, he picked up only one.

"The *Prose Edda*," he whispered.

"What did you find?" Ru had ventured into the room to stand behind Leik's right shoulder, lending his lantern's light to the endeavor.

Leik flipped pages, answering impatiently, "The *Prose Edda*. The *Younger Edda*. It's a book about Norse gods, written in the thirteenth century by a guy named Snorri Sturluson."

"I thought you hated history."

"It's not history. It's mythology."

Near the back of the book, he found what he was looking for— an image, a gruesome, black and white engraving of a bearded man shackled to a rock in a cave with a beautiful woman holding a bowl above his head. The book shook in Leik's unsteady hands. In his stunned silence, he finally heard it—a slow, rhythmic dripping.

Ru tapped the picture with a quivering finger. "Who is he?" He couldn't read the words. Leik couldn't read Icelandic either, but he knew the stories. He turned, holding the book open in his hand, eyes cutting from Lokkhart's drawn face to the bowl above him. He stepped around the man, almost slipping in stagnant water, until he could see what was above it—a suspended glass jar, full of a thick, amber liquid that dripped into the bowl through a narrow glass straw. Leik nearly slipped again scrambling back to the table. He pawed through the photos until he found the one of the tree.

"Who *is* he?" Ru's voice edged toward desperate.

Lokkhart gave Ru a wide, savage grin. "I'm Loki. Surprise!" Ru stumbled backward, indeed startled. "Yes. Our storied dungeon master, lying near dead in the other room, has determined I'm a Norse god intent on killing Baldur, another Norse god, with the souvenir arrow I bought at a Renaissance Faire for my youngest son." He cocked his head to the side. "If I were a god, would I still be locked up in these chains? Could Sven have drugged me? Oh, and let's not forget that he's the one with the Norwegian name. Sven. Sven. *Sven!* Wasn't that the name of the fat reindeer in *Frozen?* My kids love that—"

"It's the Binding of Loki from Norse mythology," Leik broke in. "In the legend, Loki found out mistletoe was the only thing that could kill the god Baldur, Odin's son. Loki wanted revenge for Odin's killing of his own children, so he crafted an arrow out of the weed and guided the hand of the blind god, Hod, so the arrow flew true and killed Baldur. Loki fled. The gods hunted him down, tied him to a rock inside a cave, and set a snake above him to drip poison onto his face for all eternity. When Loki finally broke free, he triggered the start of Ragnarök."

"Ragnarök," his uncle called from the end of the hall. His voice had become raspy and thin. "The end of the world."

Lokkhart gritted his teeth. "It's bullshit. Claptrap from the lips of a man who lost his wife to the siren song of a scoop of Cherry Garcia."

Leik continued, unperturbed. "Ragnarök begins with three icy winters, no spring or summer between them. Humans will fight to the death over food scraps and warming fires. The wolves and monsters of old will gobble the sun, the moon, and the stars. The mountains will fall. The seas will rise. Heimdall will blow his horn, and Loki will break free of his bindings and captain a ship made of toenails and fingernails pulled from the dead, and sail into battle. Almost all the gods will die. What is left of the land will sink into the sea, leaving a cold, empty void." Leik paused. "The death of Baldur and Loki's escape mark the beginning of our end."

Ru paled. "Did Lokkhart kill Baldur?"

"It's a myth, Ru." Leik held up the picture of the trailer and the tree and pointed at the squirrel nests… only they weren't squirrel nests. "This is mistletoe. I think my uncle saw it and Lokkhart's arrow and decided, in his grief, that Lokkhart was Loki. He bound him up to prevent Baldur's death and stop Ragnarök from happening. I'd guess, considering the scars on Lokkhart's face, it's not poison dripping from that jug into the bowl. It's acid." Then Leik raised his voice to make sure his uncle heard him. "But he got some of the details wrong. Loki wasn't bound by normal chains. He was bound with the enchanted entrails of one of his sons, and Loki's wife, Sigyn"—he gestured toward the bowl above Lokkhart's face— "is supposed to hold that bowl until it's full. When she empties it, the 'poison' drips on Loki's face and his screams shake the land."

Ru regarded Leik, dead serious. "There were earthquakes. You felt them."

"It's a *myth*. Sven's emptying the bowl." Leik shook his head, suppressing a horrified chuckle. He shouted, "Where are the kids, Sven? Where's his wife? Is she tied up and gagged around here somewhere?"

Sven didn't answer.

"Shit," Leik said. Worry for his uncle suddenly surged. The man had an *arrow* sticking out of his gut. He waved at Ru. "Go make sure he's okay and find your goddamned phone. We have to get them both to a hospital."

Lokkhart nearly swooned in his bindings. "Oh, thank God. Hurry. Please hurry."

Ru didn't move. He said, "I think we should listen to your uncle."

"My uncle might be dead."

"But the earthquakes…the screams…"

Leik spun around. "None of this is real, Ru. Sven did this because of Mills. He snapped."

"We might be the world's only hope."

Leik's shoulders sagged. Ru had gone and bought passage to Sven's bonkers Viking island. The luxury package. "There are no sacred herocs, Ru! Grow the fuck up! Hamilton was a player. Washington owned slaves. And Paul Revere was no lone town crier. He lied. Or maybe history lied. He was one of forty riders to spread the warning." Leik didn't think it was possible, but more color drained from Ru's face. "Look. I'm sorry. Sven's my uncle. I'm calling the shots."

Ru stuffed his jittery hands deep in his pockets. "You're an asshole, you know that?" He limped out of the room.

Spent and trembling, Leik pressed his hand against his aching side and walked around Lokkhart. In addition to the chains, a black, wrinkled rope was wrapped around the man's torso and groin and anchored to the wall under the smelly crawl space. The closer he got to that crawl space, the worse the stench, and Leik wondered if that's where all the shit went. It had to go somewhere. He found the rope's knot and pulled on it. The rope disintegrated to dust in his fingers. He heard Ru's heavy footsteps coming back down the hall as he wiped the dark, gritty dust on the front of his pants. Ru's silhouette darkened the doorway.

"He's weak but alive. He said, um…" Ru paused uneasily to clear his throat. "He said to tell you he did what he had to do."

An electric current tore through Leik's heart.

That stench.

"He said…" Ru said softly, "She wouldn't hold the bowl."

Leik's eyes panned right to the yawning hole in the wall. He held his lantern up so the cone of light bled into the shadowy space, revealing its contents. His knees went weak.

Lokkhart's tremulous voice cut through him. "What's in there? I've been drugged half the time. I didn't see—"

"Bones," Leik said, forcing the word out. He felt like he was going to pass out. Leathery skin and tufts of hair still clung to three skulls. "Human."

Lokkhart's shrieks didn't shake the ground. Instead, the wounded, starving man shook his chains so hard they left bloody grooves on his wrists.

Ru watched, anxious, from the doorway as the rest of the shriveled black rope turned to dust. "Leik, that rope could be made of—"

"Don't you say it. If you do, you're as crazy as—"

The sound of Green Day's "Basket Case" crashed the party. Tyranny. Ru's phone. Ru locked eyes with Leik, and then he turned and lurched down the hall. Leik dropped his lantern and chased after him. He had to reach it before Ru did. He had to call the cops. Get help. He slammed into Ru from behind, grabbing fistfuls of his shirt, and yanked him backward. Ru hit the floor hard, landing on his back, and Leik stumbled over him into the room at the base of the stairs.

"Don't…" His uncle coughed. His eyes were glassy. His skin too smooth. "Listen—"

"You're a monster." The words ripped out of some deep, cold space in Leik's soul. How could Sven have killed kids? How could Leik be related to him?

Green Day raged on. Leik scanned the room, his ears triangulating on the sound. In the far corner, he saw a pile of metal bowls. The bowls all had holes in the bottom where the acid had eaten through. Real acid. Real people dead. The phone lit up, pulsing in the pile's shadow.

He grabbed it, hung up on Tyranny, and dialed 9-1-1 as he

frisked his uncle for the keys to Lokkhart's chains, found them, and strode back down the hall. Ru was still on the floor, hugging his knees to his chest and rocking back and forth. Probably in shock. Leik brushed his fingertips over Ru's head. "It's going to be okay."

Leik walked into the dungeon room.

Lokkhart was gone.

"Hello. What is your emergency?"

The fragile light of the dropped lantern flickered out at his feet, plunging the close, nightmare prison into darkness. Heart in his throat, Leik whispered, "Lokkhart?"

"What is your emergency?"

From behind him, a mirthful whisper, "Thanks, love." Hot adrenaline flooded Leik's veins, and then something solid smacked the back of his head, and he was on his hands and knees with an overwhelming urge to vomit. "Oh, you'll be alright," Lokkhart said, wrapping his hands around Leik's torso and gently moving him out of his way. "Your friend—not so much."

"No…" Leik said. His head ached. His body trembled. He made a wild grab through the dark for Lokkhart's legs, but Lokkhart kicked him in the ribs. Leik landed on his side, pain shooting through his broken ribcage, lungs, and spine.

"Stay," Lokkhart commanded. Then the unbound man hummed a familiar tune as he walked out of the room, dragging something behind him.

Leik coughed, begged, "Don't…don't hurt him." He rolled onto his stomach and crawled to the doorway. His vision blurred and sharpened, blurred again. Ru cried out as a shadow bent over him. He struggled, trying to push the shadow away. Another wave of nausea and Leik swallowed hard. Lokkhart was a psychopath. He'd killed Mills without remorse, and now—

Lokkhart screamed in Ru's face, a long, hair-raising, banshee wail. This time, the ground shook. The stone walls shook. Leik's teeth shook. Dirt and rocks rained down around him. Leik pressed himself against the doorframe. He nearly pissed his pants. Ru stilled, and Lokkhart said, "That's better."

Leik heard a chain drag and rattle. The shadow stood. Ru's feet dangled. He choked and clutched at his throat. "Dear, dear, I told you to let me go."

Leik grabbed the doorjamb. Splinters pierced his skin as he pulled himself up. This was his fault. He had to do something. But the hall tipped, and Leik leaned dizzily against the stone wall. Ru's strangled sounds faded. Lokkhart dropped his friend in a heap and resumed his humming as he walked down the hall. It was a Frank Sinatra song. *I Left My Heart In San Francisco*. A bizarre choice. Sven used to sing it at the top of his lungs until his family begged him, cracking up, to stop. In the distance, Leik heard sirens. They were growing louder. Tyranny must have called after all.

His vision clearing, Leik launched himself down the hall. He stopped to feel Ru's pulse. Nothing.

"Ru, Ru..." he whispered. Angry red abrasions circled his best friend's neck. His head lolled to one side. "Oh God, I'm so sorry. So, so fucking sorry."

Ten feet away, Lokkhart squatted in front of Sven, whose breathing was dangerously shallow.

"I had…you…" Sven wheezed.

"This is for my wife," Lokkhart said, yanking the arrow out of Sven's belly, pulling a soupy mess out with it.

Leik stood and limped to the room's threshold.

Lokkhart gritted his teeth. "This is for my sons." He drove the arrow through Sven's neck. Blood sluiced over Sven's throat. Lokkhart pulled it back out, stood slowly, and turned around, fixing his sharp, dark eyes on Leik.

Leik froze.

"Shh…" Lokkhart said. He brought his finger to his lips and held the hand with the arrow up. "Stay," he said softly. *"Stay."*

Leik stayed.

The sirens grew louder.

Lokkhart turned and skipped up the steps, twirling the arrow in his fingers. Blood sprayed the wall, and Lokkhart added words to the tune he'd been humming.

"She left her eyes…in Carolina…"

LAST RITES
By J. H. Schiller

THE PRIEST TRACES A cross on the dying woman's forehead as he recites the Prayer of Commendation. "May you see the Redeemer face to face and enjoy the vision of God forever. Amen."

She shudders, gripping his metallic hand. "Thank you, Father." A violent coughing spell takes her, and droplets of blood spray the priest's dusty cassock. When the last spasm passes, she opens her milky eyes, turns her face up to the sky, and whispers, "Goodbye."

He isn't sure if she's bidding farewell to him, or to God, or to the ruined Earth, but he replies.

"Goodbye."

She takes another tortured breath, then another, and then no more. The deep grooves of pain leave her face, and she relaxes into the peace of eternal rest. As the priest rises, the servo motors in his knees grind against months of road dirt. He looks up at the roiling clouds, pondering the woman's last word.

Goodbye.

He is perhaps the only creature on Earth who knows the word is a contraction of the sixteenth century phrase, "God be with ye."

He is perhaps the only creature on Earth who knows anything at all.

With a flick of his eyes, he accesses the BioNet—the network built by the Church after the Vegas flu killed nearly half of the world's population. The virulence of the disease was unprecedented, and it mutated so rapidly that vaccines were useless before they made it to market. In the pandemic's aftermath, the UN and the WHO collapsed and smaller national governments toppled. The Church was the only global institution still standing.

Vatican epidemiologists quickly realized the key to survival was detecting and isolating outbreaks. They developed injectable nanocytes that would monitor health and report signs of potential infection to the BioNet. To convince traumatized survivors to receive the injections, the Church told the world they'd developed a vaccine. Ninety percent of the remaining population lined up to receive it.

Unfortunately, the self-replicating nanocytes caused severe— often fatal—seizures in twenty percent of patients.

Even more unfortunately, they crossed the placental barrier.

According to the priest's databases, the tragedy was accidental, but the great powers of the world believed otherwise. Tensions mounted. Sabres were rattled and eventually drawn, culminating in the Final War, which ended—in accordance with the revelations of mad John—on the plains of Megiddo where the last bomb was launched from low Earth orbit. Those hardy souls who survived both the Vegas flu and Nanocyte Rejection Syndrome ultimately fell to the war, either by instant obliteration in a nuclear blast or—like the woman he'd just prayed for—from radiation sickness.

Yesterday, the BioNet recognized one living human.

Now there are none.

The priest accesses the network that connects him to his brothers in the Order of Bezalel. Their primary directive, embedded in the very core of their governing AI, is to serve humanity. When there are no more humans to serve, their work is done, and so the members of his Order had decommissioned themselves, one by one. The last reported activity on the network was months ago. No active signals remain, save his own.

The last priest leaves the shattered pavement and walks out into a field of rubble, his black robes whipping in the vicious wind. Another dust storm is coming, and his joints are already so full of grit that movement is difficult. No matter. He doesn't have far to go. A few minutes' walk brings him to the lip of the impact crater occupying much of what was once Vatican City. The first bomb fell here, its thermonuclear yield exponentially magnified by the thousand-mile drop to Earth. Before the war, the Vatican was twenty miles inland of the Tyrrhenian Sea. Now, the priest stands in the ruins of St. Peter's Basilica, looking out over crashing waves.

It's as good a place as any. He closes his eyes and initiates a program called LAST_RITES.exe. As his systems shut down, he looks up at the sky. It was blue once, wasn't it? Despite what his memory tells him, it seems unbelievable now. The heavens above him are brown and foaming with dirty yellow clouds. Somewhere out there, beyond those clouds, beyond the orbiting machines that rained death down upon the Earth, there are stars. And perhaps some of those stars warm other worlds—worlds that didn't fall as hard as this one.

It is the stars he holds in his mind's eye as his processor shuts down.

The stars and hope.

Goodbye.

FARAWAY WAR
By Gabrielle Gold

Someone wrote a ballad in the sky tonight,

a pastel serenade no ears can hear,

but I sensed the music enter through the balcony door.

I saw the sound of the horn cascading,

a slow crescendo of rose and fire-gold

and violet, blossoming across the dim blue page.

And as quiet triumph echoes through broken clouds,

a beauty of this realm and yet beyond,

I can only imagine sunset half a world away,

where the flames and clouds that mark the end

of another day are silent, drowned by a high wail

and bursts of noise, for it is only noise, a static

that deafens eyes and hearts. The sun falls
here and everywhere, but the smoke stays, hovering
in a darkening horizon, a mirror-image omen.

Someone took raw colors, the same scale of notes,
and cast a song for us to see and recall
that where there is shadow, there is light.

THE END

DUBLIN CREATIVE WRITERS COOPERATIVE

The Dublin Creative Writers Cooperative is a group of working writers in the Columbus, Ohio area. We aim to provide a supportive and constructive environment for fiction writers of all genres and experience levels. Our meetings include write-ins, technical/craft workshops, writing contests, social events, and group critique sessions.

To join, visit our Meetup page.

Subscribe to our blog to receive updates
on our published works:

HTTPS://WWW.DUBLINCREATIVEWRITERS.COM/BLOG

Our first anthology, *Broken Promises*, is available on AMAZON

Our next published work:

DEAD OF WINTER: An Anthology
Presented by Dublin Creative Writers Cooperative

FEBRUARY 2022

AUTHOR BIOS

Marília Bonelli was born on a snowy day in Ithaca, NY. After learning the word "bus," she relocated to sunny Natal in northeast Brazil, where she grew up surrounded by far too many cats (or so everyone says). When real life doesn't get in the way, she does her best to make sense of the characters and worlds constantly trying to crawl out of her head. Her published novels include a fantastical adventure where death is less than straightforward, murder mysteries with a touch of illusion, and parallel worlds intersecting via dreams.

A. Howitt lives in a three-bedroom renovation project with a super supportive husband, four LEGO-obsessed kids, and a spoiled hamster named Cookie. She can usually be found searching for inspiration in the woods or chained to a corner desk in her bedroom where she often eats and sometimes sleeps. Her favorite writing tools are colored pens, sticky notes, dry erase markers, a day planner, magnets, and a folding lap desk that fits in the bathtub.

J. H. Schiller grew up in the Blue Ridge Mountains of Virginia—a real-life coal miner's daughter. After traveling the world from home to Hangzhou, she settled in Ohio with her husband and children. She writes speculative fiction and recently completed her second novel.

Anne Johnston is the pen name of a recent escapee from the strictly non-fiction world of academia now writing contemporary and speculative fiction. Her debut anthology of short stories, *Wish Upon a Pocketwatch*, is available on Amazon, and she is currently working on the first book of her Lamplight Series. Anne works in the thrilling world of state government and statistics and lives in Ohio with her husband and mother. When not at her day job or busy writing, Anne spends time contemplating the tricky nature of life and wishes from her kayak. Find her on Instagram @annejohnstonwrites. Website: **https://annejohnstonwrites.wixsite.com/author**

Gabrielle Gold is a creator at heart. She started writing stories, poetry, and songs in high school, and has never stopped. In 2011, her short story "Hidden Brilliance" was published in Across Town, an anthology curated by the Columbus Creative Cooperative. She has earned awards in songwriting contests at science fiction and music conventions and is currently working on a high fantasy novel. When not writing, she loves singing, trying new foods, tabletop roleplaying, obscure online research, and talking to her jade plants. The plants tolerate her presence well enough.

J. Levesque writes poetry, personal reflections, and fiction. Her poetry chapbooks *Haiku* and *Simmer* are available on Amazon, as is her COVID-19 memoir *Isolation: A Journal*. Her science fantasynovels *Dominion of the Lost* and *Dominion of the Hidden* are available under her pen name, Jora Dublinn. Her work can befound at **jlevesque.website** and **joradublinn.com**.

"*Thomas Brown*, don't you turn your back on me, damnnit! Where will you go, what will you do?"

"I'll go to Ohio, I'll write whatever genre grabs me. You know, none of it's real. But you can find me at **tbrownlbtf@gmail. com**," I said as I showed the deadly blond my back, taunting her, playing with fire.

I heard the quick motion of her hand and turned in time to see her throw the black blade at me.

Light danced off the keen edge as it cut through the air on the way to my eye and…

Cody Bok has a Ph.D. in I/O psychology and works in corporate HR at JP Morgan Chase & Co. He writes short stories while trying to appease his needy cat, Pearl.

Autumn Shah writes in the suburbs of Columbus, Ohio. She lives with her husband, two teenage girls, and a pandemic puppy who has been a godsend. Her fiction has won local awards, and her creative nonfiction has been published in several literary journals. You can read some of her writing at: **https:// myshamelesswonder.blogspot.com/**.

Stephen Woodfall is a mysterious writer, musician, and generally creative weirdo, with a lifelong appreciation for speculative fiction, especially fantasy. He lives on his own in Northern California, and likes movies and novels, games and silliness. He loves sushi, but can't always afford it. Fortunately, he likes Mexican food, too, and he can usually afford that. Other details about him are closely held secrets that may or may not come to light in time.

Valerie George, MD writes out of nostalgia for her hometown in the Appalachian foothills—the ghost-tour river city of Marietta, Ohio—where it is said that there are more dead than alive. She studied creative writing at Vanderbilt University and has since embarked on a lifelong mission to write stories that merge the mundane with magic and small town gossip with sweeping legend. She currently resides in Columbus, Ohio, where she is completing her radiology residency and fulfilling her dream of sitting in dark rooms, writing, illustrating, and enjoying the quiet company of her parrot, Paloma.

L. H. Adamkiewicz is a published author and experienced freelance writer, currently living in Northeast Ohio. In her free time she creates social media writing challenges, like the 5 AM Writer's Challenge and the Stephen King Writing Challenge.

Find Leigh here: **www.l-h-adamkiewicz.com**

Twitter: **@LioFromOhio**

Instagram: **@LeighWillWriteThat**

J. Powell Ogden lives in Dublin, Ohio and graduated from The Ohio State University (O-H!). She writes horror, science fiction and young adult dark fantasy. She is also the CEO and creative director of Spark Street Media, LLC, a small press publishing company. Find her here: **www.jpowellogden.com** & **www.sparkstreetmedia.com**.

Made in the USA
Middletown, DE
27 August 2023

37251873R00165